After the Gold Rush

After the Gold Rush

Stories

Lewis Buzbee

Tupelo Press
DORSET, VERMONT

ISBN-13: 978-1-932195-38-5
ISBN-10: 1-932195-38-6

First paperback edition May 2006
Library of Congress Control Number: 2005911083

Tupelo Press
PO Box 539, Dorset, Vermont 05251
802.366.8185 • Fax 802.362.1883
web www.tupelopress.org

Cover and text design by Howard Klein

Cover painting: *Palmer Avenue*, oil on canvas by Rick Monzon
www.rickmonzon.com

Acknowledgments

"Hairpin" first appeared in *Capilano Review*; "Beauty" in *Warren Wilson
Review*; "Five and Dime" in *Black Warrior Review*; "An American Son" in
Land Grant College Review.

For Julie and Maddy

The coolness of the riverbank
the whispering of the reeds
daybreak is not so very far away.
Enchanted and spellbound
in the silence they lingered
and rowed the boat
as the light grew steadily strong.

—*Van Morrison*

Contents

Red Weather

The world was blue and quiet when Robert woke. For a very long time nothing moved, then he heard his mother scraping along to the kitchen where the light snapped on and the thud of the heater kicked through the house. He heard the rasp of a wooden match and knew his mother had lit a cigarette. A few minutes later his brother Gene wholloped out of bed, rustled into his clothes and slammed down the hall. His mother murmured something to Gene as he entered the kitchen. He whooped and was out the door, gone down the street. Then it was quiet again, only the soft breathing of the heater.

Robert pulled the quiet around him, balling deeper into the blankets. He knew that this would be the last of the quiet, the space between now and the moment when his father returned. Although he had been whirling anxious for days, he wanted to drown himself in this last moment.

"*Deserta*," Robert whispered, "*deserta*." This had been his secret incantation for the last year, and he had used it to invoke his father every day and especially at night. Before his father left, Robert sat with him in the big chair in the living room, the atlas opened to a yellow country surrounded by blue. "*Arabia deserta*," his father told him, a desert. Drawings in the map's margins showed caravans of camels, pink cities, men in tents, scorching sun. Robert had breathed the word *deserta* as if it were the one link between his world and the fabulous desert. This morning Robert blew on the word when he whispered it, sending his father home over the vast miles of parched desert, past the men in tents and the camels and the pink cities, blew on the word until his father tumbled onto the front steps of the house, home at last.

The quiet pushed heavier on the house now. Robert slid out of bed into his slippers and glided down the hall to the back door. The world was blue. A blanket had been tossed over it, blue and quiet as far as could be seen and known. Mount Uhmunuhm was covered with the blanket, and although the oak trees tore through the blanket in places, they had also turned blue. The telephone wires were blue, and the fences, and the things that Robert had left in the yard the night before, his bike and a ball and some guns, all smothered by the blanket.

The blue cracked under his feet. Some boys were yelling on the next block, or maybe many blocks off, but their noise was so distant and muffled it was a mere reminder of what noise had been before the blanket had transformed the world.

The blue burned in Robert's hand when he bent to touch it, and it burned on his tongue when he tasted it, sharp, cutting. Every time he breathed, the blue air filled his nose with shiny crystals. Two blue birds swam to a perch on the bare, blue branches of the cherry tree.

Robert's mother stood behind him.

"It snowed, Robert," she whispered from behind the screen door, as if she were afraid to frighten the blue away. "It never snows in California, honey. You're very lucky to be here and see this. You'll be able to tell everyone that you saw snow in California."

She took a drag from her cigarette, then steamed a long cloud of blue smoke. Robert jumped from the top step into the yard. The snow covered his slippers. He turned and smiled, waiting for her applause.

"Come in, honey," his mother said, opening the door and flicking the cigarette into the yard. "We'll get you dressed, then have some breakfast, and you can go build a snowman."

Robert wore his racecar pajamas under rolled up jeans and a plaid shirt. His mother put two pairs of socks on him, his tennis shoes, his rain boots, and his yellow slicker. In the kitchen Robert sat at the table and watched the blue outside. His mother made breakfast with a burning cigarette in her left hand. She stirred his cocoa, which he sipped as greedily as he could. His mother served him a plate of raisin toast smeared with butter and topped with cinnamon. She had baked the toast in the oven so that the cinnamon blackened, crunchy and sweet; the butter and the raisins and the toast were soft and warm. Robert ate all of it.

"Your father will be home any minute," she said, brushing her bangs away from her eyes. "You better go out and enjoy the snow now. But stay in the yard."

The world was still blue, but less so. Mount Uhmunuhm was still blue, but on the far side of the valley, very far away, where the hills were without trees, red came into the sky, and above this red, traces of gold. The houses at that end of the block were white now.

Gene was playing with the neighborhood teenagers. Some were building a snowman, while the others ran around it, pelting one another with handfuls of loose snow. They screamed and clattered, breaking the silence with their angular arms and legs.

Robert looked back at the house, but his mother wasn't in the window. He saw that the places he had stepped in crossing the yard were bare, his footprints exposing the grass, stealing the snow. He also saw for the first time that snow was not blue, but white, the white taking over everything except for the big piece of red on the far side of the valley. He was suddenly hot, bundled up to his chin.

A purple and gold taxi turned down the street and drove honking past Gene and his friends, and as it pulled up to the house, Robert's mother came to the porch, shivering in her robe, holding herself, rocking a bit and whispering. The taxi was lighted inside, and although Robert saw only his silhouette, he recognized his father, the way he talked to the driver. For a moment the quiet of the morning returned, his mother silently whispering, Gene seeming to holler faraway down the block, and his father telling a joke behind glass. Robert listened to his own breathing, and in that quiet, his breathing was as loud as his breathing when his father had taken him diving, the only sound in the world his own breath.

Mac had left for Arabia the year before, to dive for oil companies after his retirement from the Navy. Robert had been full of questions about diving before Mac left. One day Mac took him to one of the Navy's testing pools at Hunter's Point, where he strapped a triangular mask to Robert's face, a Jack Brown mask. Robert and Gene had been in water since they were babies, so Robert was not afraid of the water that day, but he had been frightened by the mask, feeling suddenly cut off from the world. He struggled, trying to shake his head out of the mask, like a dog shedding a hat, but Mac grabbed the mask and held it steady, looked into Robert's eyes, saying nothing, and made slow breathing motions until Robert fell into the same rhythm. The cool oxygen filled his lungs, and he smiled at his father. The air in the mask tasted like pennies. Robert lowered his face into the water, and guided by Mac, swam in circles. They didn't stay long. The whole time there had been the feeling that what they were doing was forbidden.

In the weeks before Mac left for Arabia, he and Robert sat together in the orange chair and looked at the atlas and talked about life in Arabia and what type of work Mac would do. Robert listened intently, glancing up occasionally with a knowing look that chastised his father for going too far in his stories. Robert had been underwater and did not believe in sea serpents or water witches.

In the first weeks after Mac left, Robert could not believe that his father was gone; he expected to find Mac in the house when he came in from playing. His father's chair smelled of his aftershave and cigarette smoke; Robert would sit in the chair and inhale his father. But as the months went by, his father faded and became crabbed writing on crinkled sheets of blue paper Robert's mother would read aloud at the dinner table. Robert began to suspect that perhaps she herself had written the letters from Arabia. The letters were tedious, with no mention of the fantastic adventures Mac had dreamed up. At night in bed Robert tried to conjure what his father looked like. In the morning Robert would go to the television set and look at the framed picture of his father in his khakis against a backdrop of white sand, black ocean, and palm trees. Even that picture began to seem wrong.

Now Mac was in the taxi in front of the house, and Robert tried very hard, squeezing his eyes shut, to imagine his father's face once more before he saw him.

The moment his father stepped out of the taxi, Robert ran at him and was instantly up in the air, wheeling around, looking down at his father, shocked to see that his father's hair had mysteriously turned white. Mac lowered Robert to his face, still turning, shouting, "snow, snow, snow," and Robert smelled his father's smell and knew then that he had truly returned.

Mac turned Robert upside down and laid him on his back in the snow, both of them laughing, then he stood and took Olive into his arms, cupping his hand around her head and pulling her close to him, the both of them laughing, then kissing. Robert lay on his back and waved his arms along the ground, raising slushy waves of snow.

Gene screamed in from nowhere and landed on his father's back. Mac swung to face him and for a moment they played at wrestling, stalking each other, but then they embraced, and everyone was laughing and talking at once about the snow and Mac and the taxi. Olive lifted Robert off the ground, Robert playing dead weight, and pulled him up onto her hip. The taxi driver in his purple jacket and gold hat leaned against the morning and watched, sucking on a toothpick.

Mac paid, and the driver opened the trunk. Gene pulled out two canvas duffel bags, but before he could toss them aside, he gasped. Mac and Gene both bent over the taxi and extricated a worn leather sea chest. The taxi drove off into the morning.

Gene and Mac hauled the sea chest into the master bedroom with Robert standing to one side, wanting to help. Olive came in with a cup of coffee for Mac and sat next to him on the bed. Robert and Gene sat on the floor, the rugged chest between them. Mac sipped from the chunky mug.

"Let me just look at you all," he said. The house closed around them for a moment, embracing them, just the four of them, the family, with no snow or screaming children, no taxis, no Mount Uhmunuhm, no *Arabia Deserta* thousands of miles away.

Olive let out a little cry and fell against Mac's shoulder. Gene punched Robert.

"Everyone will be here in a couple of hours," Olive squeaked through her tears. "For breakfast."

"Presents, then," Mac said, kissing Olive on the forehead and lifting her off of him. "Have I got presents for you?"

They had always been an occasional family, Christmas and birthdays filled with presents. The last Christmas had been even more overloaded with toys and clothes. Olive tried to make up for Mac's absence with ribbons and boxes and bags. On those days during Mac's absence when Robert became upset and demanded that his father return, Olive soothed him with a reminder that his father would surely bring home presents. Once, during the summer, Gene and Robert sat on the porch late at night and speculated what their father might bring them. Robert had imagined that the presents his father brought from Arabia would be very much like those he got at Christmas, but when Robert saw the trunk he knew that these gifts would be of a different order. He sensed that these presents, hiding patiently in the massive chest, would not disappoint the way others did, the toys pale imitations of what he saw in his mind as he ripped at the colorful paper. The mystery of the trunk, where it had come from and where it had been, consumed Robert. It had once been a pirate's trunk, of that he was certain.

"But first," Mac said, cracking open his zippo. "Let me tell you about Arabia."

Mac held the cigarette poised over the floor, while Olive leaned back and retrieved an ashtray from the nightstand.

"It's as big as you can imagine," Mac said softly. "Bigger than this whole valley, bigger than California, by a long shot. It's all desert, sand and sand and sand. But the water. The clearest most beautiful water in the world, and I've seen all the water now."

Mac paused and looked out the bedroom window, where the day was brightening, then got on his knees, bent over the chest, and carefully loosened the frayed straps that held it shut. Mac's tan had reddened and deepened, as if Mac had absorbed the Arabian sun directly into his skin, scorching himself. Robert stared at the tattoos on Mac's upper arms where they crept from under his short-sleeved shirt. There was a hula girl on his left arm who danced when Mac flexed his biceps, and on his right arm an anchor. Robert reached across and touched his father's tattoos.

"Is everybody ready?" Mac asked in a television voice.

"Wait, wait," hurried Olive, her hands searching the bed and the pockets of her robe. She lit a cigarette and nodded.

"Harash!" Mac growled.

This word was round and guttural, grinding, and in it Robert heard the sound of the sands being blown along in a storm and the creaking of the saddles of the camels.

The chest lay open. On the very top was a brass plate as big around as the chest could hold. Mac held it up. Hammered into the plate were scenes of Arabian warriors in full armor. The brass was highly polished, but blackened with age in the crevices. Spears and lances raised, brave knights charged across the plate on swift, fierce steeds.

"A feasting plate," Mac said. "Dates, jack fruit, star fruit, exotic fruits you can't believe; spicy meats, cool sauces. I bought this in the bazaar, but I ate off one just like it at the home of a prince. We ate in a tent in the desert. There were dancing girls. Just like in the movies."

Mac passed the plate to Olive, who examined it closely, then set it down behind her.

"It's beautiful, Mac," she told him, then she waited for the next treasure.

Mac unraveled a wad of paper and pulled a velvety red hat from it and put it on his head.

"A fez," he said, crossing his arms and shaking his head so the golden tassel danced about.

"Ain't never going to do it without my fez on," Mac continued in a funny, singsong voice.

From a beaded and mirrored bag Mac poured a stream of silver and gold coins in front of Robert, who tried to decipher their crazy, wiggly writing, but Mac was soon pulling other things from the trunk. Green earrings for Olive, pointy leather shoes, wallets, headdresses, cans of food covered with the same wiggly writing as on the coins. The trunk was bottomless. At first Gene and Robert were proprietary of everything, asking Mac to divvy up the goods, but after a while the abundance and splendor proved too much for them to keep up with.

Mac produced a bag of sea shells that he himself had found at the bottom of the Red Sea. Robert kept a collection of shells from all over the world, most of them gathered by his father from the oceans he had dived. These Arabian shells were completely strange to Robert, twirled delicately and encrusted with tiny beads of blue and yellow and purple and green. Robert was unable to fathom what sort of fantastic creatures had lived in them, except to imagine that they must have been fragile and lacy, different from the fleshy lumps that he had seen evicted from other sea shells.

Treasure covered everything. Robert could hardly move for it. Everyone talked over one another, trying to catalog and describe it all. Mac had brought gifts for everyone in the family, aunts and uncles and cousins. Nearing the bottom of the trunk, Mac pulled out four bottles of amber liquid. The bottles were thick, curved like the trunks of manzanita, and he laid them carefully on the bed. This drink, he told them, was from a secret oasis and made from pomegranates. Mac handed a tiny parcel to Olive and winked at her and then at the boys and said it was Olive's special gift for later. Olive blushed. Then Mac unwrapped a curved leather scabbard from which he drew a long, half moon knife.

"This is an assassin's knife," Mac said, staring at Gene. "It was carried by Arabian soldiers for secret missions at night. You will need it one day."

He threw the knife at Gene, who reached up instinctively to catch it, but the knife flashed by well above him, where it stuck in the wall with a heavy thunk.

"Mac!" Olive yelled, her face frozen between a smile and a scream.

Gene drew the knife from the wall with anxious reverence. He turned the flashing knife blade before Robert, careful to keep it from his reach. Engraved on the knife's handle and blade were the same writhing characters as on the plate and the coins. A thin gutter edged the blade, which Robert knew was for the blood of the enemy.

"Well," Mac said, pounding the inside walls of the empty chest. "I guess that's all, nothing more in here, all out of presents, nothing special left for anyone else."

Robert was crushed, even though he knew that he shouldn't be. Any moment his father would bring something from the trunk that was especially for him, but he also felt that the waiting might destroy him. Robert looked away from everyone.

"Yep," his father said. "I guess that's just about it. I can't seem to find anything at all in here for anybody else, just pretty much an empty box, but wait—"

The long heartbeat—Mac did find something in the last corner of his chest.

"Why, what's this?" Mac asked, pulling out a leather camel the size of his hand. The camel was adorned with a saddle and mirrored bangles. Mac handed the camel to Robert, who pulled it to his chest and then threw himself against his father.

Robert put on the red fez and marched around the room, giving commands in gibberish and open sesame talk, driving his camels across the burning desert. Mac played the camel, and Robert climbed onto his back and drove him around the room.

Olive lit a cigarette and called for calm because company would be coming in a while and there was work to be done. Mac urged Robert and Gene out into the snow, everyone almost having forgotten it. Mac closed the bedroom door behind Robert and Gene. Robert was about to explode from it all—the abundance of the morning—so he attacked his brother, grabbing his legs and calling him a big fat camel driver. Gene dragged him across the living room and out into the snow.

℮

Robert and Gene tried to build a snowman in the front yard, but the melting snow in the sharp sun would not stick to itself. They wandered the blocks of their neighborhood looking for snowmen, hoping to stumble on a snowball fight, but all the snowmen had melted and everyone had gone inside. The day tired. The roofs of the houses splashed water on the lawns and sidewalks, and the streets gurgled with braided streams of thaw. The earth steamed.

Turning the corner to their block, Robert saw his cousins' cars parked in front of the house, surrounded by a buzz of people. He took off running, while Gene walked behind him, dragging a long branch. Robert weaved into the knot and went straight for his father, leaning into his leg while Mac talked to crazy Uncle Charlie.

Robert was the youngest of the eleven cousins, the children of his mother's three sisters, and except for him, they were all teenagers. Robert was everybody's favorite, too young to hit and too old to ignore. He was also small enough to scoot around and in and out of the crowd, noticed or unnoticed as he chose. His aunts and uncles patted him on the head and said hello in high-pitched voices, and his cousins tried to cajole him into playing, but Robert was content at that moment, standing next to his father, the sun warming everyone.

The party moved indoors where tables and TV trays were stretched from one end of the dining room to the far end of the living room. Olive worked in the kitchen with her sisters, who had brought along bags of dishes and bowls of food wrapped in tinfoil.

Noise filled the house like water poured into a cup. Robert put his fingers to his ears and pushed them shut over and over, making a strange babble of the clamor, as if the adults spoke a desperate, dangerous language. The heat had built up over the morning and in the warming day had suffocated the house, so the doors and windows had been opened. Robert imagined the noise rolling out of the house and into the streets, where it was swept away by the melting snow.

Uncle Charlie called on everyone to sit down so they could get started, but no one listened. He chimed a glass with his spoon, and still no one listened.

Mac yelled for everybody to sit down. The room stilled, then Mac shifted to a sweeter tone.

"My lovely wife, Olive, here," he pronounced with a broad wave, "she has prepared for me a tremendous homecoming breakfast, and she's ready to serve, and I say we all get quiet and pick our places now because if you're not careful, you'll end up sitting next to Uncle Charlie and you won't be able to hear my fabulous tales of Arabia over his story of the last crazy thing he did."

Everyone laughed and clapped and made quickly for a

chair, except for Uncle Charlie who stood waiting next to the television. When everyone was seated, he took a seat delicately on an ottoman in the corner of the living room. Charlie raised a glass of water in toast, but no one paid him attention. The long table sank deep in a noise of clanking glasses, forks, and plates. As the meal progressed and the eating became serious, a deep silence infiltrated, punctuated only by exhaling and chewing.

Robert looked up from where he sat near his father at the head of the table and made goofy eyes at his cousin Lori, who made goofy eyes at the rest of the family. Then Lori oinked a pig noise, very quiet, but her sister Meri heard her, and she made the same noise, then Gene heard and they all burst out laughing, and once again the house succumbed to the maelstrom of the gathered family.

Olive scurried back and forth from the kitchen to the ragged, uneven line of tables. The breakfast was a special one, prepared only on the most auspicious occasions. Though Robert begged for it almost every Sunday, Olive had fixed this breakfast only once during the year Mac had been gone, on Mac's birthday. Along with juice and coffee, and bacon, sausage, hash browned potatoes and coffeecake, there were two slices of toast on every plate. The toast was cut into one-inch squares onto which Olive spooned a thick sauce with chunks of hard-boiled egg white in it. Then, and this was the best part Robert thought, the hard-boiled yolks were grated finely over the sauce, the gray yolks turning bright yellow when they were pushed with a spoon through a sieve. Olive sprinkled paprika on top of it all. Robert loved the thick, gooey mess of it, though he never managed to finish his mountainous portion.

"Mac, honey," Aunt Marie asked quietly enough for everyone to hear. "Why don't you tell us about Arabia?"

Mac stretched back in his chair and took a deep chug of coffee.

"Well, now," Mac said, lazy. "I'm not sure that I can tell all of it with our present company."

He winked at Marie and looked down the table at Robert and the teenagers.

"But I'll try," he said.

"In Arabia I met a man who asked me if I wanted to play dice with him. I said yes, and he pulled out his teeth, five gold teeth, each shaped and marked like dice. He rolled out his gold teeth right there in the dark alley. I let him win for a while, then I beat him. When we were done, he spit on his teeth, wiped off the dirt, and put them back in his mouth."

Mac looked away as if the corner of the room were a telescope trained on that place and time.

"I was diving oil rigs, mostly repair, nothing too exciting. Once in a while we'd have to recover a drowning victim, but otherwise, it was barnacle scraping time. One day, though, I'm diving a rig and I see this big, white thing coming at me. At first I think it's a beautiful woman, floating along in her robes, calling to me. Sometimes you lose contact down there. I start to swim towards her, almost feeling her lips, but then I finally see that it's a jellyfish, a twelve-foot Man-o-War, and I know I'm in trouble."

No one was eating. Mac got up from the table with his coffee cup and went into the kitchen. A cupboard opened, then there was the sparkly sound of glass on glass. Olive dropped her fork loudly and looked to the ceiling as if it were heaven. Mac came back to the table, sipping his coffee, not missing a phrase of the story.

"I turn and start to swim away as fast as I can, but that jellyfish is coming right after me."

He paused, gulped his coffee, sighed and continued.

"Then I feel the most god awful burning sensation you've ever felt, like electric needles, all over my body. It has me covered, twelve tentacle burns."

Mac turned to one side and lifted his desert-colored shirt. There were three scarred splotches on the side of his stomach, each as red as a sunset.

"The rest are on my legs and one on my shoulder."

"Is that what turned your hair white?" asked Charlie with a sharp stick in his voice.

Mac looked up at the ceiling.

"Yes," Mac said, "I think that's what did it. I do think you're right. It was the Man-o-War that did this to me. Changed me for good."

Mac smiled, lit a cigarette, sat down and crossed his legs.

"Yep," Mac said. "Things were never quite the same after that."

The cousins were a blur of questions, Mac answering rapidly with a yes or a no or a shrug, but he seemed at the same time to retreat from the questions and fall into his coffee cup more and more. He had stopped eating and sat back in his chair, rocking on its hind legs, drinking his coffee and smoking, one arm around Robert's shoulder.

When Charlie asked Mac a question about spitting camels, Mac ignored him, but a glint came into his eyes and he let the chair fall towards the table.

"I want you all to see something," he said in a voice that was too loud and wrong for the room, as if it were a piece of another conversation from somewhere far away.

"Robert!" Mac announced. "Get the fez!"

Robert felt an urge to look at his mother, as if she had tugged a piece of string tied to his chin. The newness of this day had worn off, and it seemed to Robert that they were all living through a day that had happened many times before. Olive stared at her plate.

"Robert!" Mac yelled. "I'm talking to you, you bum. Now go, my favorite son, and get the fez that your sailor of a father has brought to his quiet home from the four corners of the world."

Mac was laughing, and so was everyone else, but the laughter of the cousins and aunts and uncles was hollow, like the clattering of bones. Robert paused, watching, then slid underneath the table and crawled through a forest of legs. He bolted to the bedroom, followed by a gust of fresh laughter.

In the bedroom the lifeless treasure was strewn across the floor like dead Army men. Through the short winter light that poured into the bedroom, Robert noticed that his camel looked particularly tired and had already lost some of the stuffing in its neck.

"Robert!" his father yelled. "Get your fez in here."

Robert stood before the vanity mirror. The red and gold fez fell over his ears and eyes, but by pushing it back on his head, he found that it stayed tight. He began to spin, and the gold tassel of the fez turned as perfectly as a helicopter's blade.

"Sim, sim, alla bim," Robert intoned under his breath. "I shall now fly away."

He smiled at himself in the mirror and paraded back to the family feast, his arms crossed genie fashion.

"Sim, sim, alla bim," Robert said in his deepest voice.

Everyone laughed and clapped.

Robert spun his head slowly again, until the tassel flew, then he put his arms out to the side and made an airplane noise as he zoomed around the tables.

"It sure beats flying carpets," he said.

The table cracked up, the laughter like popping corn. When Robert passed by his father, Mac grabbed him and hugged him too tightly and pulled him onto his lap. Mac whispered something to Robert, while everyone else shushed and tried to hear. Robert smiled and went straight to Uncle Charlie.

"This is Genie," Mac said across the tables to Uncle Charlie. "The one with the light brown hair. I brought him back from Arabia with me. He shall grant your fondest wishes."

"Sim, sim, alla bim," Robert said, twirling the fez's tassel. "You are not crazy anymore."

Even Uncle Charlie laughed. Robert turned to look at his Aunt Marie, who was patting him on top of his fez. Robert shrugged off her pats as only a truly dignified genie would.

"Sim, sim, alla bim," Robert said, nodding at his Aunt. The fez fell down over his face. "You are not married to a crazy man anymore."

The table drowned in laughter, except for Uncle Ernesto who sat still with a mysterious half smile on his face. Robert went to his cousin Lori's chair. She cast a solemn expression and waited for Robert to speak. He pushed the fez back on his head, but said nothing.

"Well?" she asked.

"Well, what?" Robert said. "You tell me. I'm just the genie here. I can't do all the work."

Lori pulled Robert to her, but he squirmed away.

"Wish, slave!" he commanded.

"I want Jimmy Rodriguez to ask me to the Valentine's dance," she said, embarrassed.

"Great genie say yes," Robert said amid a howl of screams from the cousins.

Robert went to everyone at the table and granted their wishes. When he came to his mother, she wished that Gene would be the best baseball player on the team for the upcoming season. Robert paused deliberately and looked at Gene who stared back at him until the wish was granted. Mac wished that his favorite son Robert would return, and Robert waved his arms all about until the fez fell off and he yelled Ta-Da! and was Robert again. Everyone clapped and fell to teasing Lori about Jimmy Rodriguez.

"Well," Olive said loudly. "I think I'm gonna make us some more toast. Who wants more eggs *á la* goldenrod?"

The table came back to life. Robert stood next to his father's chair while Mac and Uncle Ernesto talked about oil prices. Robert watched his mother at work in the kitchen. She attacked the breakfast.

A quick thud shook the house, then a shower of sparks filled the kitchen and sprayed into the living room, silver light everywhere, the lights flickered, and everything was both brighter and darker than it had been the instant before. Olive screamed, and Mac was out of his chair. The sparks died and the lights came on again, but there was a blue fire around the toaster. Olive's housecoat had caught fire on the sleeve; Mac hugged it to his chest and it went out. Aunt Edith was running at the toaster with a pitcher of milk, but Mac stopped her just as she was about to pour it. Uncle Ernesto tossed a throw rug from across the room, and Mac smothered the fire.

"Well, folks," he said. "That's it, show's over, no more breakfast this morning. But thanks for coming by. We'll see you all next year."

The morning broke into pieces. The cousins went out to play in the slush, the men sat in the living room drinking coffee and smoking, and the women cleaned up the tables and the dishes. Robert wandered among them all. His Aunt Judy pulled him aside while she loaded the good dishes in their zippered containers. She asked Robert to please make a genie's wish for his Uncle Ernesto who was very sick. Robert chanted his magic words.

By noon, the short, sharp light had melted all of the snow except for brief traces under the evergreen trees. With no snow left to play in, Gene and the teenage cousins talked about the snow while they stood around various cars. Robert weaved in and out of their legs, listening to their talk and deciphering it, singing along to their songs on the radio. The oldest cousin, Chuck, tall and thin next to Gene, was going into the Marines in less than a month. The talk centered on what life in the Marines would be like and where Chuck would be stationed, followed by cool silences in which the cousins tried to imagine life in the world. Chuck, boldly smoking a cigarette and combing his greased hair, hoped for embassy duty, maybe Burma, where a friend of his was stationed, or somewhere else in Asia. Everyone thought that sounded too neat and nodded silently to show their approval, smoking hidden cigarettes.

A black-nosed military plane passed overhead, making its arduous, curving ascent over the peak of Mount Uhmunuhm. These planes passed overhead every two minutes of every day, even on Christmas. Mac had told Robert that these radar planes circled the Pacific hunting Russian submarines.

Olive and her sisters came out onto the porch, marveling at the day and its unexpected warmth and clarity. Marie yelled at the kids that that smoke had better not be coming from the lungs of her daughters. Her middle daughter, Meri, turned and waved and told her mother not to worry, then turned back to the group and exhaled three perfect smoke rings.

At the far end of the street, Robert saw a figure coming towards them. The figure walked with the casual deliberation of someone who had been walking for days and had some far way to go yet. The man's gait reminded Robert of his father's. A duffel bag rode the man's shoulder; he walked with his hands in the pockets of a thick, blue coat.

Robert ran to his mother and pointed to the man. Olive looked down the block, squinted, then shaded her eyes with a dishtowel. She inhaled sharply, hissed, and bolted into the house.

Gene looked up to see the figure, and recognizing it, ran at the man, who held out his arms as if he were catching a basketball.

Mac shot out of the house and stopped on the edge of the porch, where he stood with his feet wide and his hands on his hips. The man, who stood at the far end of the yard hugging Gene, pushed him gently aside and looked up to Mac.

"Chief!" the man yelled.

"Nin! You old son of a bitch."

Nin. There was always talk of Nin in the family, but to Robert this person was simply a name. When Robert asked questions about his uncle, Mac always answered brightly and quickly and promised that someday Robert would meet him.

The hush into which the homecoming had slipped broke, and everyone maneuvered to shake Nin's hand and shout questions at him, everyone at once. Only Olive hung back, leaning against the doorjamb and wiping her hands on her ragged dishtowel. Robert leaned against her legs.

The crowd around Nin parted at Mac's command. Nin came to Olive and kissed her on the cheek, then he backed up and looked down at Robert. Nin put out his big hand.

"You must be Robert," his uncle said. "I'd recognize that Macoby grin anywhere."

Robert broke into a tremendous smile.

"Robert," Mac said, kneeling next to his son, one hand on his belly. "This is your uncle, Nimion Divine Providence Macoby. But you can call him Uncle Nin."

Robert's smile was huge, but he managed somehow to swallow it. He pulled his hand away and crossed his arms.

"Sim, sim, alla bim," he chanted. "Give me an uncle named Nin."

The laughter returned as a flock of birds, then the group broke and pushed into the house, Gene dragging his uncle's duffel bag.

Nin looked almost exactly like Mac. He was a little older, more wrinkled. His skin reddened into a tan that was the same depth as Mac's, but where Mac's was red all the way through, Nin's tan was brown and dusty along the edges. His uncle looked like a cowboy. Mac's hair, now white, had disappeared mostly from the top of his head, but was still thick on the sides. Nin's hair was completely gone, revealing a veined skull. Mac's eyes were gray, Nin's dark brown with orange flecks, but both men had the same droopy eyelids, the same hooked nose, the same high, rounded cheeks, and the same mouth, a mouth capable of a sly, round-the-corner smile or a toothy, inviting grin. The brothers sat next to each other at the table and talked as fast as railroad trains passing. They ate up the air between them. Robert sat on his mother's lap and watched the men talk, but was unable to hear over the din.

Nin motioned Gene to bring him his bag and gestured to someone behind Robert for glasses. Nin pulled two bottles of clear liquid from his duffel and pounded them on the table. Mac applauded and laughed and pushed his chair away.

A tray of glasses was set before Nin who filled several of them and passed them on to the adults, then he splashed a couple of sips into the rest and passed these to the teenagers. A glass was set before Robert, but before he could get to it, his mother emptied it into her glass and moved them both out of Robert's reach.

Mac raised his glass.

"Nin," he said. "Where the hell have you been, you old bastard?

"Chief," Nin said, clinking Mac's glass. "Everywhere. I've been everywhere. Every god damned where."

The two men stared at each other and drained their glasses straight off. Everyone else at the table tried to keep up, coughing and gasping for air. Nin refilled the glasses. Robert tugged on Olive's sleeve until she let him have a whiff of the white lightning. The smell of the liquor coursed into Robert's lungs, bright and astringent. Robert shivered.

Uncle Charlie tapped two glasses together until there was quiet.

"A toast," he said. "To the two weary travelers. Home at last."

"Amen," Olive said.

Amens chimed from everyone.

"Listen, everybody," Nin said, standing. "I've got a big surprise for you all. Now, I know it's impolite to bring unwanted guests, especially when you might be unwanted yourself, but I met the two most amazing women on my way here, and they're waiting down the block in my car. I didn't really walk all the way, you know. I want you all to meet them. And I apologize to our lovely hostess," he said, gesturing to Olive and looking sheepish, "for this inconvenience."

Nin waved from the front door. Olive bobbled Robert on her knee, while everyone else fell into loud whispery chatter.

"*Señors, señoras, señoritas,*" Nin announced. Behind Uncle Nin, Robert spied a rustle of colors, wild birds pacing a cage.

"Today," he said, bowing a little and smiling his sly, slow smile. "We have for your entertainment an unparalleled excitement. Direct from the Caribbean, may I proudly present, and ask you to give a warm Macoby welcome to, Conchita and Manuela."

Nin drew himself aside. Two tall, muscular women entered the house. Everyone clapped. One of the women was the color of melting chocolate, the other the color of the sun, Robert thought, if the sun were as black as oil. The women wore identical outfits of multicolored cloth strips, orderly bunches of bright rags. Their skirts dropped halfway to their knees, their tops covered their breasts, turbans wrapped their heads. Each woman wore chunky bracelets, each bracelet a solid, shimmering color—purple, green, yellow, blue. The two women stood there, smiling wide and open, flashing white and pink mouths. They shook the hands of those nearest them. Robert noticed drops of sweat on the curious ripeness of the woman with the oil- and sun-black skin.

Mac poured drinks for the women.

"Welcome," Mac said and raised his glass. "Friends of one are friends of all."

Mac and the women gulped their drinks, and everyone else, nursing their glasses, nursed them a little more bravely.

Nin opened the console stereo in the living room and flipped through the stack of records. The needle dropped with a thump into the groove and found scratching sounds; beats of a low drum were followed by tinny horns. The women began to shake, talking now in a curious tongue, moving away from the table to the center of the living room. Nin stood with one hand on his stomach, the other hand snaked in the air. He danced in place with himself as he watched the two women.

Conchita and Manuela gyrated in the middle of the living room, rotating towards and away from each other, and revolving around each other, like slowing tops. They made clacking noises with their tongues and short, sharp yelps through closed lips, while they shimmied and slowly bobbed up and down. The dance was languorous and breathless at the same time.

The women beckoned to Mac and Nin to join them, and the men danced a mock version of the real dance. The song ended, and everyone in the room, including Olive, applauded. The two women bowed deeply and were offered fresh drinks.

Robert jumped from his mother's lap, put on his fez and stood before the two strangers. The next song began, and Robert shook his shoulders and moved his hips and threw his head back as the women had done, and soon Robert fell to the floor, helpless with his own laughter. "Very good, very good, little man," the darker woman whispered to him. Robert's father picked him up and hoisted him over his shoulder like a sack of potatoes; Robert saw everything in the room as if it were minute and within his grasp. The dance started again, and now everyone in the house— cousins, aunts, uncles—danced.

Robert whirled from person to person, half-blinded by the red and gold fez. Nin and Mac stood to one side and talked. Manuela and Conchita showed the teenagers how to move. Gene took charge of the record player, and the songs grew faster and louder.

Olive poured coffee from a silver urn and served squat slices of a cake she had baked. The cake's frosting was pale green with pink lettering that said, "welcome home, daddy." Robert snuck two pieces. The cake was white on the inside, spongy and without flavor.

Manuela and Conchita asked Gene to find them a slow song. The cousins sat on the living room floor and ate their desserts.

The two women faced each other, and as they slowly circled, they moved in and away from their center, calm as waves. Their hands hovered away from their bodies, circling birds. The tempo of the song stayed constant, the dancers at no time doubling it, but there was an increased urgency as the dance evolved. Robert noticed that as the women pulled towards each other, then away, that they stayed together longer and also stayed apart longer, each returning and leaving more intense. As the even rhythm of the song built to its climax, the eyes of the dancers brightened and grew hungry. On the very last beats of the song, the dancers drew close again, but this time they did not stop and pull away; they stayed on course until their sweating bellies touched, then their rag-covered breasts touched and then their mouths. The tongue of one dancer reached out and swallowed the tongue of the other, and the dance ended with the women kissing deep and insatiable.

The applause broke around Robert like bright coins floating in the hot air, but before he could wrap himself in the noise, his mother grabbed him by the arm and dragged him to the back of the house, screaming, "everyone, get out of here right now." Robert felt his mother's hand shaking, and he could see the rage flying from her head. Then Robert heard a thick pounding at the front door of the house.

"What the hell is it now?" his mother screamed, letting go of Robert, running back to the living room. Robert followed.

Mac signed for the telegram and tipped the delivery boy. Everything had turned to silence like thick water. The dancers hid behind Uncle Nin.

"Give me that," Olive growled, snatching the yellow envelope from Mac's hands.

She tore open the telegram, read it quickly, then her face paled, and she handed the yellow paper to Mac.

"It's Dad," Mac whispered to Nin, no trace of his voice in the words. "He's dead."

Mac handed the telegram to Nin who read it again, and said only, "oh, boy."

"What?" Robert asked in the silence.

Olive gave Mac a tired, quick hug, then gently took Robert by the hand and led him down the dark hall to his bedroom. She sat him on the bed and bent over him, looking into his eyes.

"Robert," she said. "You just stay here for a while, please. Some bad things happened in the other room, and we have to take care of them. Stay here. I'll let you know when you can come out."

Robert sat scared on the bed. Into the window the evening peeked blue and still. Under the silence Robert heard the sound of voices, low and ashamed, the clicking of shoes and the shuffle of coats and purses. Everyone was leaving in a small hurry. When the front door shut, the tiny calm was broken by screaming, then the screaming collapsed, and the front door slammed, then the calm returned but on uncertain, wary feet, hiding hunched in the corners.

Robert played camels across the dunes of his unmade bed, distracting himself long enough to let the pieces of the broken day fall around him. He went to the door and listened. He slowly turned the knob, hushed the door open and found the hallway dead as skeletons. Yellow lights burned in the living room and kitchen, bright and still.

His father and his Uncle Nin sat alone at the kitchen table, their elbows propped up and scrunching the dirtied white tablecloth. The three of them were alone in the house. The clear bottle, its clear liquid, and the two glasses shone sharply in the evening light. Outside the blue dusk was shot through with green. Robert leaned against his father's chest. Mac put his arm around him and drew him close. Uncle Nin reached across the table and ruffled Robert's hair.

"Haroun Al-Fazar," Mac said tenderly, his voice lighter than air. "My favorite genie, my very favorite genie."

Mac took a long draw on his glass, then looked out the window to someplace not across the street. Robert knew that his father looked far out across the sea from the bridge of a ship or across the desert from the back of a camel.

"We had a little trouble here today, Haroun," Mac said, kissing the top of Robert's head. "But everything's gonna be fine, you just wait and see. Your mom just got a little hot; she'll be back. That's the hardest thing about leaving, Haroun, coming back. You better get used to it."

"Yes, sir," Robert said in a low genie voice.

"Good genie," Mac said. He turned back to the table and slapped Nin on the shoulder.

They sat at the table while the evening gathered quickly around the house and prepared night's soft nest. Nin told Mac of his adventures in America, where he had been for the past five years, and why he hadn't been in touch. Mac asked him if wouldn't stay with them, for good. Nin shrugged. Mac told Nin about Arabia, including a story about fifty Greek sailors who chased him over a steel fence. Mac raised his shirt to show off the four-inch scar on his back, and the splotched scars of the jellyfish. Robert fingered the ruptured skin.

After silent drinking, Nin spoke.

"Do you remember him?" he asked, looking away.

"I was only ten or eleven when he left," Mac said. "That's what I remember, but I can never keep anything straight. I get Oklahoma and Modesto mixed up all the time. What about you?"

"I remember too much," Nin said, drinking hard. "I always have. Here's to the old bastard, wherever he is."

"Wherever," Mac said, falling into the quiet.

They rose, each carrying a bottle, and they lumbered like bears to the easy chair and sofa in the corner of the dark cave of the living room. Robert turned off all the lights in the house except for the one in the stove hood that he could not reach. His father and his uncle slept immediately. Mac yelped softly in his sleep, his foot jerked. Robert imagined that his father dreamed of chasing tigers across the desert.

Robert slipped into the front yard. The air was oddly warm. Last night's snow, which had disappeared so fast, had made the ground wet and odorous. Robert smelled the valley soil, rich and black in his nostrils, as thick as if he were chewing it. Night had descended except against the western wall where, above Mount Uhmunuhm, a vivid streak of red sky beckoned.

The day had been too much. Robert wished he could separate it into different days, the way the sky divided itself into colors. The snow, his father, the treasure, the feast, the toaster, his uncle and the dancers, the telegram, —any of these would have been enough for one day. He would have to try very hard to remember it all.

Hairpin

In that long still moment after the crash, I knew that Halley was already dead and that Ella wasn't, and I was filled with rage that Halley would leave us. Ella was unconscious but breathing. It would turn out that Halley wasn't officially dead yet, she would survive three days of intensive care in a Greek hospital where the staff's English was so perfect they could describe every detail of her condition to me. Waiting for help to arrive on that hairpin curve, I knew Halley was gone, that the envelope of time that was my wife had already been sealed. I did not speak any words aloud in our overturned rental, the silence there was too immense. Instead I seethed, cursing Halley for leaving us alone, for allowing me to be the driver and the one who'd killed her and almost killed Ella, for those long years of empty afternoons Ella and I would have to face together. I hated Halley then and don't know that I'll ever forgive myself.

What little I remember of the crash and the moments before it doesn't really matter. Banking into the hairpin turn, downshifted and whirring, there was suddenly another car in our path, a blue car coming right at us and the knowledge that the crash was going to be bad. I've been told we flipped at least once. We bellied up against the stone guardrail. The Aegean, the bright hole of the sun, the blue car flipped over the guardrail and tumbled into the sea, the driver dead. The doctors and police tried to tell me about the driver, he was old, but I didn't hear much.

Ella and I both had broken legs, simple fractures, and Ella had a deep gash below her shoulder blade, and for days we were both bruised and shocky from the impact. We shared a room and that was good, she's only nine. Ella woke me up in that room a few hours after our arrival, whispering, Dad, Dad, Daddy. I crawled back to the world, remembered the crash, turned to Ella and whispered, It's okay, Chuckie, it's all going to be okay, your mom's fine, we're here. She turned from me, smiled at the ceiling, and fell into an improbable sleep. The bruise on the side of her face glowed against the mint green of her blankets, and I stared at her for as long as I could that morning, trying to remember the colors in that room as if it were crucial that I did. I thought I should call someone, probably Halley's sister, but fell asleep.

Our doctor was a big man with hairy hands and knuckles. He came in twice a day, winked somberly at me when he crossed the room to Ella's bed, then he'd sit with her for several minutes, talking to her with his back to me. He'd inevitably pat her arm. The only phrase I ever decoded from their conversations was during his first visit. Ella had risen on her elbows and was staring at him. Superbly, he'd said, absolutely superbly.

When he was done talking with Ella, he'd come to my bedside and give me a stern look before he spoke. Well, he'd say, we better get you down there so you can cheer up that lovely wife of yours. Verbatim, every single time. Two orderlies would wheel me down the hall, the doctor walking alongside and looking directly ahead, telling me about Halley's prospects, serious but possible, going over details of friends and relatives they'd contacted. At the end of each trip, he'd say, Be strong now for Ella, then he'd look at me once and go off on his rounds.

I thought I should talk to Halley during these visits, but found we no longer needed words. It wasn't that I knew she was dead already that kept me from speaking, rather the sense that our lives had become too concrete for words. She was a ghastly version of herself, to be sure, blue, nearly transparent, still she was Halley. After these visits, I would be transported back to the room where Ella was waiting, and the orderlies would push my bed close to Ella's and I would tell her that her mom was going to be fine and so were we. When she asked me why her mother was in another room I told her there were complications, and that seemed good enough. The orderlies would separate our beds and Ella and I knew it was time for sleeping.

Halley died near one in the afternoon, quietly they told me. It seemed an odd hour of the day for a quiet death, so many buses and cars outside. I knew something violent must have moved through her. I saw Halley's body one last time, then the orderlies took me to Ella and left us alone. I told her, Your mother's dead, Ella, she died peacefully. I know, she said, I know, I know, it's going to be okay. She was smiling. She stared at me, her hand on mine, then after a moment, she turned from me to the green wall, twisting her shattered leg, and finally cried. I put my hand around her as far as I could reach. I tried to explain to her why I had lied about her mother's condition, and she told me she knew, she understood everything. We spent the next two weeks in that same room in the hospital, tended by Halley's sister.

We've been back home for three weeks now and most of the hoopla is over and things are quieting down. Halley is not buried but scattered from an urn at Ocean Beach, quite illegally, Ella and I would like to believe. The friends and relatives have been through and are getting back to their lives. The casseroles are nearly gone, the counters piled with clean Tupperware that will have to get returned. Ella and I are glad to be alone, we're exhausted from the sympathy.

It was the end of August when we flew back from Greece, a season of wet day-fog in San Francisco. Our flat was warm and dark and it was hard for us to get out. At first we both walked with sleek polished steel canes, and we were told to take it easy, we were still brittle after all. Between pods of visitors, we made ourselves take short walks, once around the block, forays into the park, out in the cold long enough to need to go back inside, but yesterday Indian summer came, warm and too bright, and we know we have to get out more, see what comes next.

❧

I keep expecting to see Halley on the street, not her exactly but someone who looks exactly like her. I've been preparing for this moment since we left Greece. San Francisco is full of women who look like Halley, at least from a distance. Hiply dressed, thin to the point of wiry, hard to pin down the age, twenties to forties. Halley was thirty-seven, dark glasses, mop of curly hair pulled tight in a bun. You might never guess she was a mom. I look for these women now and keep looking, hoping to be shocked or hopeful or bereft. Turns out no one looks like her any longer.

I'll tell you the trouble with the dead, my friend Kenny said one evening last week. Ella had a ton of homework, or so she said, but was really, I suspect, leaving me alone with Kenny because she thought I needed it. She impressed us both with the knowledge that fourth grade homework was heartbreakingly difficult, a bear, she called it, and literally skipped down the hall to her room while Kenny and I settled into the quiet of the evening, sipping bourbon as was our habit when we were together. Kenny is a poet, a very good one, which you might imagine without knowing if you spent an evening with him. He sits quietly, watches and listens, sips his drink, he always has a drink, then he speaks in a near stutter, his words colliding. The halting breathiness of his voice makes me want to weep the way Charlie Parker makes Kenny want to weep. I usually do most of the talking, some blather or other, but not this night, I had spoken too many words since bringing Ella home.

The trouble with the dead, Sam, he said, they aren't dead, the dead just won't die.

No, Kenny, I told him after two sips of his bourbon, the trouble with the dead is that they are dead, forever, gone, *no màs*.

What could he say? I held the trump: my grief.

We spent the evening talking about Halley's clothes. She was a fashion designer, loved clothes, but she never took that world too seriously. I've always suspected Kenny had a crush on Halley, a feeling that has deepened since his divorce a few years back. Listening to Kenny talk about Halley's style, especially the way he remembered a pink and black fur coat she had, the way he described that coat with his hands, I knew for sure he had been in love with her. Loved her, does. A good thing.

Much later that same evening, Ella came out of her room and begged Kenny to put her to bed. I was asleep on my own bed before they had finished their storybooks. I was ashamed of what I'd said to Kenny that night, how I'd flatly denied a central vein in his poetry, and how I made it impossible for him to argue his truth. I fell asleep because I couldn't bear to face him, but I had to tell him what I absolutely knew. The dead are gone. Even in a town where she was so common, I couldn't find Halley. No ghosts, no specters, no shades. Simply removed, absent.

❦

Ella sleeps a lot. The minute she gets home from school she naps through the bright afternoon and into the long river of evening. She sleeps on the red couch in the front room with the traffic outside and seems as small as a toddler. I have to wake her up for dinner, some dish I've heated. While she sleeps I work in the spare room that is my office. I work at home, architecture, these days a pretty light in-box, and each day I hurry through my projects certain that this afternoon I'm going to take my daughter out into the sun but she's so tired. Around four or so I get up from the desk and go into the kitchen and do the dishes, then sit at the island to do the crossword and drink a glass of wine, only once in a while going into the living room to watch Ella sleep. I have to say she looks great these days, even sleeping, healthy and rested and flush, and her hair is shiny. She sleeps burrowed in the crease between the seat and the cushion, in sweatpants that were her mother's and that she only wears for these naps. To watch her breathe while she sleeps makes me feel that she is safe and doing the best she can for herself.

We eat dinner and talk, mostly about her mom. We talk all the time about it, no, about her, about Halley, and we're always interrupting each other with, remember the time. We talk a lot about Halley when I pick up Ella at school and we walk home together, the light of these afternoons perfectly burnished and stretched for such talks. *Remember the time,* we start.

Sometimes Ella tells me that she doesn't want to talk about it, just had a bit too much, she says, can we get back to that later, and on the weekends we'll watch a movie or we'll read together, the windows opened and the offshore breeze pushing in, the one season we get these warm winds, and we won't talk about her mother at all, and it's a relief for both of us, we know. Ella's right, there's only so much, but still I think we're doing pretty well, and we even talk about that. They, however, tell me she's not doing well in school, and I don't know what to say to that.

Kate Shamblin calls, she's not even Ella's teacher, a concerned parent, mother of Pablo, a boy Ella has invited to her parties. We've known them the way one knows people in this town, everybody only three or four years in, few real connections yet, passing through. Halley and me, we're old timers, ten years. Ella, lucky girl, was born here. Appears Kate and Mrs. Jouthas, Ella's teacher, have been talking and they both agree that Ella is much too quiet. They mean well.

Sam, Kate says on the phone, sounding as if she's about to make the apology of the century. Sam, I know it must be hard and to be honest with you I'd rather not butt in but Ella's being so quiet these days, don't you think. It's not good for Ella, Kate and Mrs. Jouthas and a few interested others have suggested, for Ella to be that quiet. She should be talking it out, processing, progressing up the steps of grief. When they ask Ella how she's feeling about her mother, Ella shrugs and says she doesn't know then says she guesses she's sad. When they ask Ella if she misses her mother she says, Yes of course, and gets, well, a little curt. Almost everyone believes that Ella's holding in too much, maybe she needs some help. Kate was wondering if the four of us couldn't get together, her me Ella and Pablo, maybe take a walk. Maybe Ella would open up to her.

Ella doesn't like to walk, she likes to do things and she's furious with me for agreeing. She can smell a rat a million miles off and knows she's being set up, sniffs pity in the air. We make a deal and she relents, apparently I'm going to buy her something. I don't know why I've agreed to this walk in the first place, I have a very short leash these days, and being out of doors for more than an hour makes me a bit crazy. I said yes to forestall any further butting in. Ella and I wait for the weekend with a slightly pleasurable sense of dread. Saturday morning the heat is already fierce when Kate and Pablo show up at our door and pry us outside.

Kate is an attractive woman, but she has odd gold streaks in her hair, and she dresses, Halley always said, as if she were still trying to please her father. A thought half crosses my mind that Kate is here for me rather than Ella, but this is such an unseemly thought it goes nowhere. On our stoop Kate gives Ella a hug that's much too big and long. Pablo is standing on the sidewalk, his face bored beyond repair, his feet endlessly at work. He's a sweet kid and he's as gracious as he can be greeting Ella and trying to strike up something of a conversation. They talk about school and race out in front of us. A short skinny kid, he has to look up at Ella when they're talking as if she had all the answers he'd ever need. We shoot into the park toward the playground.

She's adorable, Kate whispers to me, it's so sad for her. Yes, Kate, it is, so sad. Which is the only and most obvious answer and I'm bored with speaking it, and even Kate can tell I'm bored with it when I try to fake it, but she smiles anyway and we go on talking, only I'm wondering rather perversely if this woman would be as concerned as she seems if Ella weren't as adorable as she is.

Kate speaks at some length in earnest tones of Ella and her silence, and I agree that it's troubling but I want them all to know that we do talk, she does, and we're taking it as best we can, remember, I tell her, we were in the accident, too, our bodies in the same car, a certain recuperating from physical damage alone. By this time we've reached the carousel park, Kate and I are sitting on a bench under a great Modesto ash, while Ella and Pablo look for something to do. It's beastly hot, the hottest day yet, close to a hundred I'd say, and the air has decided to be as still as it can, we'd call it earthquake weather but out here we're a bit superstitious of that turn of phrase. It seems like nothing is moving though it's Saturday and the park crowd is giving it their best shot. Ella and Pablo are sitting on swings, their feet firmly planted in the sand, and they're miserable, suffering the assumption that because they are children they must play out in the sun.

Pablo is turned away, Ella is facing us. She leans way back in the swing, as if she might at any moment tumble off, and she's smiling at Pablo and laughing at what he says, she's flirting. I can't help but smile at this, then Ella catches me out and her face falls quickly grim, closed, and she pivots on the swing, her back to me now, the chains tangled, and I'm nearly undone.

Sam, Kate says, have you thought of getting help, asking for help, seeking help. Yes, of course, I tell Kate, and it will come, look, help is coming, but be patient with Ella, she does know what she's doing, but let's change the subject. I tell Kate all about me, how much I miss Halley, how hard it can be to simply walk down the hall some days, and I'm lucky I have Ella because she gives me someone to care for, the imperative of her, and how that, too, turns out to be painful because there's so much of Halley in her, but this is bearable. I don't really tell her anything at all about Halley. I keep going.

Finally, I can no longer watch the kids suffer, Kate, I say, let's get them out of here, get some ice cream, it's just down the street, we could all use some cooling down. At the ice cream shop, Pablo and Kate do astute imitations of their teachers, and never go over the top, like they might have last year, or six months ago. They're growing up, it's plain, and Kate and I take our quiet satisfactions in watching them. Ella pulls a pitiful frown, nearly canine, a perfect shot of Mr. Crappuchettes, yes, his real name, a school counselor she's rather fond of, and I burst out laughing, and everyone else is laughing, and I say, Kate, see, look, we're laughing.

Ella slugs me in the arm real quick, unseen, as we're cleaning up our plates and mugs, and we lock eyes for a minute. Yeah sure, I nod back, we can end this now, and I say, Pablo, shall we escort the ladies to your car, and we do, and Kate and I make promises to keep in touch, and they drive off into the hot, bright day.

Back at home, Ella heads straight to the couch, too hot to change into mom's sweats, and drops off immediately, so I go back to the office where it's too hot to do any real work, and stare out the window and find myself still a little furious with Kate. I know I'm being both defensive and self-righteous but I can't help myself.

Ella and I have at least five more hours of daylight, and while I love to gaze on the ragged back gardens of our block, after a while I'm roasting and think maybe I'll nap with Ella in the front room in the shadowed half of the flat. She's not asleep after all, she's sitting in the window bench watching the cars and trees outside and keeping a close eye on the sidewalk below her. I stop at the far end of the dining room, I can see her from here, and watch her for a bit, she's quiet and without any expression other than concentration. I know what she's doing, I think, I think she's building a city inside of herself, a new city on the foundations of a lost city, and there are some doors in this city that she will not open, but she's putting them there and knows who lives in those houses, and the inhabitants are mostly memories of her mother. It's a big city, big enough for now, but hilly and curvy, and she's even putting in some dark alleys she knows well enough to stay away from, but she's also put in lots of sunny plazas and ornate houses with cobblestone courtyards, and there are many festivals in the evenings of this city she's building.

The light in the flat reminds me of a day when Ella was about two, a gray oasis of shade. I think Halley was gone, out of town on business, she did that a lot for a while, and Ella and I almost always had a great time, went lots of new places. This particular afternoon, though, I had let Ella get the best of me, and before you knew it, I was all het up and grouchy, and she wasn't going to stop standing on the couch, that was clear, and so I made it worse, and for the first time ever sent her to her room where she was to spend an hour alone, and even at the time I felt like a bully. To top it off, a gorgeous day. I called it quits after three-quarters of an hour, and knocked on her bedroom door, where she was playing with her animals in a most civilized fashion, which made me feel more guilty. Let's go someplace new, I said, and she jumped up as if nothing had happened, and I took her to Castle Toys, a store in a neighborhood we hadn't visited before. The day got saved, and the light then was just like the light today.

Want to go to Castle, was all I had to say, and Ella really did smile, still looking outside, then turned and said, sighing, not Castle again, just like her mother used to every time the two of us lit out together.

I find it hard to know if the store has changed much, Ella and I have come here so often since the first time, but it seems about the same, small and cramped, filled with bins and set-ups and boxes, and very dark and empty this Saturday, cool, nearly chill. It has always been our tradition to come here to play with the trains, wooden sets from Finland that only Castle seems to sell. They've got a great, huge mountain and village set up in the back. Today Ella goes right to the trains and begins to string the cars, and makes me tell her the story of why we first came here, this is a tradition, too, and I have to tell her about the time her mother wasn't there and I got mad at Ella but we got over it and had a great day anyway.

We get a little carried away, keep crashing our trains together, running off the rails right into the middle of the little village, all clamor and havoc, knocking over fences and trees and signs, and running into shops and homes, and I know we should be more quiet, but there's no one else here, and besides, we really are enjoying ourselves.

Beauty

We talked all through the afternoon. I'd come by to say hello and found her alone in the house. She was taking a shower when I rang the bell, I could hear the water running, and she came to the door wrapped and turbanned. After she'd finished drying and had dressed, she made coffee, and we sat in the living room. Her husband and son were out, doing something in the world, and we took time to catch up. Afforded the luxury of the time alone and the comfort of the warm house, she began to tell me stories from her past. I sensed, as we talked, she sipping her coffee and then arranging the cup carefully on the table with her small hand, that she was telling me stories she had not told anyone in a long time, perhaps had never told. I also sensed that she had a need to tell them, though I could not guess why. There was no plan to what happened; it was the shape of the day.

One day in college, she told me, a boy had asked her what it was like to be beautiful. This was during her freshman year. She and the boy were in her dormitory room; he lay on her bed, and she sat at the mirror brushing her hair. They weren't doing anything really, barely speaking. She thought they must have been pretending to study. Classes were over for the day, and they had not gone to dinner yet. Perhaps she had been getting ready for dinner. It must have been early autumn, still hot and dry, for this had happened in the first term, and she remembered that the evening was still at a distance. The afternoon was spacious.

The boy, she knew, had not been coy in his question. He had asked her what it was like to be beautiful, with all seriousness, which was unusual for him. They had spent most of their time together laughing, he making her laugh. He was very funny. When he asked the question, there was in his voice an understanding that she was beautiful, and she had agreed to the premise, not protesting, as she would normally when her beauty was mentioned. Her mother had taught her to be demure in this. It was the lack of coyness in his question that allowed her to accept his assumption. It wasn't at all like when other boys mentioned her beauty, as a tease, like bait. He might have been asking her a question on the fall of the Roman Empire or the structure of a freshwater nudibranch for all his matter-of-factness. The boy could only have seen her back from where he was; she could see his feet in the mirror.

She stared at herself in the mirror, her brush stopped mid-stroke and held next to her face. She told him, plainly, that she didn't know, but the tone of her voice when she said she didn't know, neither questioning nor denying, implied that she had only been unprepared for the question; she would need time to think about it. He had been the first person to ask her about something she had often thought on but had never spoken of. She resumed brushing her hair. She didn't think that she ever answered his question.

The same boy had come to her room the first week of the term, they had met already and talked some, to ask her another question, his first question. Would she, he asked, be his friend? On that day he had been quite formal, nervous, they hardly knew each other. He sat backwards on a desk chair facing her where she sat cross-legged on the floor reading a newspaper. She wore a scooped neck shirt and knew the boy stole glances at her breasts when she looked down at the paper. She told him then that of course she'd be his friend. She didn't know at the time, she told me, that the boy was in love with her. She didn't know how she could not have known that.

They talked all afternoon and ate together in the commons that evening.

She did not know what had become of the boy. He had left school after two years. They exchanged cards and letters for a while but lost touch.

That second afternoon, when he'd asked her what it was like to be beautiful, she told me she knew then that the boy was in love with her, and also that she and the boy would never be lovers. They would never be lovers because the boy had found her beautiful, and as close friends as they might become, there would always be a barrier between them, his mention of her beauty, the way he said it and stood outside of it. She had felt this barrier between herself and other men before, and would again.

She stopped talking, looked out the window, then laughed, holding her hand over her eyes. It must sound awful, she told me. It's not that she herself thought she was beautiful, she wanted me to know. That was not the point. The point was that men and others had always told her that she was beautiful, acted toward her as if she were, something they wanted from her.

She got up from the chair and took our cups to the kitchen to get more coffee. When she returned, she sat and looked out into the yard; she held her coffee cup in both hands and blew on it, considering.

"Why do you think he felt," I asked her, "that he had to ask you to be his friend?"

She told me she didn't know. The boy's questions had made her anxious at first. She felt as if she possessed something he wanted, and the desire for friendship on his part was a thin disguise to get whatever it was. But the boy never pressed her on anything, never confessed love for her, made no overtures other than those of his awkward friendship. He was more afraid than she was, she realized at some point, but she was too young to know what to do with her power and didn't think she even wanted it. No, he would never have hurt her.

One time she did catch him unaware. They had been at a party together, and she had, she remembered now, acted rather brazenly and foolishly. Rash. There was another boy at this party, and she thought she might be in love with him. This other boy was tall and quite lovely, a geologist. He was sure of himself. She and this other boy had spent most of the party together, talking, flirting. She touched the buttons of his shirt while they talked. She was attracted to him, was covetous of him. She and this boy stood close; he talked to her of the need for an ecological consciousness among the masses. She looked up at him with bright, excited eyes, and she was, at the party, fascinated with him, found his every word charged with passion and intelligence. The minute she left the party with this boy, her ardor thinned, and walking through the campus in the night, her mind snapped clear by the ocean breeze, this boy seemed only what he was, a lovely boy, clumsy in his self-importance.

While she stood there flirting, she caught a reflected image, in a mirror or a window, of her friend, the boy who had asked her about her beauty, and she knew that he had been watching her and the geologist for a long time. The boy held a drink in one hand, his other hand in his coat pocket. He was looking at her. When she realized the boy was watching her, she was embarrassed, but that passed quickly, and she felt instead disturbed by her friend's gaze, as if he owned her. No matter what, there would always be this barrier. No matter what, he would always know more about her, from his watching, than she would know about him. She would always be looked at.

She stood and asked me if I'd like a drink and went to the kitchen. I heard running water and the clink of glass. She returned with reddish drinks in small tumblers. We sat quiet. She sipped her drink and let her head fall back. The living room was small and informal. She sat in the corner farthest from me, in an overstuffed chair, her legs drawn up beaneath her. A plane of light from the western window hovered between us, mote-struck. The light passed closest to her so that occasionally her bared knee broke the light and shone. The light was both shade and halo. Outside was crisp autumn, cooling.

How could she explain to that boy what it was like to be beautiful? She was unable to tell him how it disturbed her to be looked at like that. She couldn't explain it. She wanted to know how we'd even got on the subject.

While we talked that afternoon she kept telling me to listen. Listen, she would say, listen.

e

She had five sisters, she told me I knew. They were all beautiful.

Each one of them had, at one time, been too beautiful to someone. A younger sister, and the one she'd always been closest to, was very beautiful. Perhaps she was the most beautiful of all the sisters, and as far as could be told, was nearly ruined by her beauty. No, she had been ruined by it.

When this sister was in college she met a man who was struck by her beauty and set out to court and win her. The man was wealthy, connected to the unversity through his money. My friend thought the man had been generous to the university as a way of meeting beautiful young women. He took my friend's sister to his large house in the foothills above the ocean and offered her a world she'd not known before. He impressed her with his objects. She was determined to stay in school and finish, and she did; even the man wanted it that way, he told her. He told her that he did not want to interrupt her life, only that she share his. He rented her an apartment near the university, where she studied during the week, and on weekends went up to the house in the foothills. Sometimes during the week, he would visit her and spend the night, but mostly he left her to school and her friends. Summers, he took her on short vacations. She worked and took summer classes, occasionally went home for a visit, had friends and went to the beach, but most weekends went to the man's big house. The big man's house. He never met any of her friends, and he did not meet her family until the wedding. She hardly talked about him. He was twenty years older than her, though still young enough himself. She agreed to marry him. He was a man of great patience. She graduated a semester early.

The sister became a beautiful, rich, young wife. Just like that. One day, there was no more student apartment filled with cheap rattan and wicker furniture. She had let the man rent the apartment for her and buy her clothes and things, but she had insisted on furnishing her rooms herself. And then she was living in the big house. Even though she'd spent her weekends there for three years, it was different now. It was her house. The man allowed her complete freedom within the house, and she filled it with objects of great elegance. She became fond of a certain type of small, ebony sculpture and placed these cool forms on white pedestals in every room of the house. The sculptures were simple gestures, a tree, a wave, a panther's leap. The ebony seemed perfect moments caught, she used to say. She rid the house of practically everything the man had owned before. Her husband was pleased.

Just like that, my friend said about her sister. Just like that. One minute she was an art major, the next she was busy possessing. She'd fallen off her other world.

At first the sister was occupied with being introduced to the man's circle of associates. My friend met some of them after her sister married. Older men, beautiful young wives. Soon the sister grew bored, and my friend was often invited to come and stay with her. My friend was living far from the university at the time, in the small house where we now sat and talked, but her sister paid the plane fare. Her sister took her shopping; they bought clothes mostly, and once when they were together, a new piece of ebony sculpture. My friend was shocked at how much money her sister spent and found it difficult to accept her gifts. But my friend was even more shocked at how, on these trips, her sister seemed so changed.

One day, shopping for underwear, the salesgirl, a rather plain young woman, still in college probably, had been unable to find the proper size. This was at a classy store in an overly formal mall, granite and running water. Yes, the underwear was expensive, silk and French, but the sister had no reason to act the way she did. The salesgirl was just doing her job, not being mean or stupid. You little bitch, the sister called her, and then she pushed her other purchases off the counter onto the floor and walked away. My friend stood speechless at the counter, wanting to make an apology, but the salesgirl simply shrugged and picked up the underwear.

When my friend caught up to her sister at the elevator, she noted an air of propriety in her sister's face, a correctness, but there was also a fear under this composure. The elevator rang and opened. Her sister asked my friend if she wouldn't like to get something to eat, some dessert perhaps.

These visits were tiring, and one weekend, my friend made excuses at the last minute and did not go. The next time they saw each other was a year later, at Christmas, a big family gathering, all the sisters and the one brother, spouses and kids, cousins, aunts, assorted orphans. They had rented a big cabin in the mountains. Snow and everything. Her sister had come alone, her husband preoccupied with business. The family was proud of the sister, adoring of her. They exclaimed her beauty, equating it with her successes in the stupid, unthinking, irresistible way families have about such things, avoiding the unspeakable by heaping words upon it. Individually they talked behind her back, worried, little hissings everywhere. She denied them their exclamations. She told everyone about her new clothes; they were rather rare. She brought gifts for everyone, and they loved them, babbling above their embarrassment. The gifts were much too fine for them. It used to be the gifts she gave were all cheap little toys, nothings from a Five and Dime, but always perfect. A green frog that spit a sticky and obscene red tongue. My friend still had it around somewhere.

Christmas just sat there, uncomfortable in a stiff chair and smiling to beat the band. No one was having any fun. It wasn't a family thing; it was about the sister. Politeness reigned. My friend watched it unfold with a silent horror. She was shocked at the arch appearance of her sister. The clothes she wore were flamboyant, magazine stuff, padded for deficiencies. Her make-up a thick copper mask. She was unable to see her sister's beauty any longer. She wanted to talk to her, longed to say something honest to her about anything, even the impossibilities of saying anything honest. But she felt that the slightest breath of truth would set the house on fire and drive them all, half naked and in their bathrobes, out into the snowy night, the children screaming and everything ruined.

My friend wondered, only briefly, what the man thought of his beautiful wife now. Then she put the question from her mind. She had never liked the sister's husband and did not care what he thought.

That Christmas she couldn't have had time alone with her sister, even if she had found the words that beat around her heart. Her sister orchestrated everything. She was either not in the house, or surrounded by everyone. She lived in the kitchen a lot, a good way to attract a crowd. Then she'd be gone, and no one knew where. If you've ever been in a big cabin like that in the snow, stuffed with people, you'll know. It's no privacy, or snow. Someone will always find you.

Here was the thing. The day before everyone was to leave, she found her sister about as alone as she would ever find her. With the husband of one of the other sisters. Most everyone had gone out for one last walk. My friend had stayed behind, and watching them leave, noticed that her sister was not among them. She began to look for her sister, hoping they might finally talk. She looked without calling to her, out of respect for the hushed cabin, and soon fell under its spell. It was the quietest the cabin had been all week. A trail of silence led her from one room to another. It drew her down the hallways and drafty stairwells. She loved the creaky floors under her feet. It was real silence. Then the hoarse animal noises. It had never occurred to my friend, she wasn't thinking of it at all, and she couldn't be sure what the noises were. She opened the door. It was that simple. She didn't see them clearly, but knew, closed the door and went out for a walk of her own. She wasn't shocked at what happened, but was shocked at what pain her sister must have been in. The incident was never mentioned, according to the holiday's rules. She still doesn't know if her sister heard or saw her that day.

The next day at breakfast, suitcases everywhere, her sister pulled her aside and whispered excitedly that she just had to come visit her soon. She had a big surprise. The next autumn my friend's sister tried to kill herself, although no one in the family claimed to know why. She had been so fortunate, they all said. My friend tried to go see her sister then, but her sister's husband said over the phone that everything would be fine. She needed to be alone, was all; it was a freak thing and under control. The next spring the husband left the house and found another house and another beautiful young wife.

They rarely saw each other now, she and her sister, usually at safe and loud family gatherings. She was worried over how much her sister drank and why she seemed so removed. She couldn't believe she was telling me this.

e~

My friend excused herself for a moment and walked deeper into the dark house. I sat in the living room. Outside it was turning evening, the sharp autumn sky preparing to leave itself to darkness, glowing white-yellow at the horizon, blue and purple in its domes. It was lovely.

When she returned she filled our drinks and sat down across from me. She tucked her legs beneath her again and curved her shoulders against the chill. I noticed how small she was.

She did not know, she told me, why men felt they had to possess.

"What do you mean?" I asked her.

She told me it was like the boy in college, the one who had asked her about being beautiful, the feeling she'd had that he wanted something from her, that barrier between them.

When she graduated from college, she told me, she took a job at a gas station. She didn't really know why she had taken the job, except that she had no idea of what to do, and perhaps there was some resistance in her choice, a resistance to being instantly married or saddled with a silly career. She only worked at the gas station two months, but it was great fun. She wore a uniform with her name on it, and they had a bowling team.

One day a man came to the station and spent too much time dawdling over the transaction. He asked her to check the oil, the water, and the air. It was a real gas station, window cleaning and all. The man seemed much too interested in what grade of oil might be best for his car. When he handed her his charge card—had he used the card so she'd see his name?—he asked if she was interested in children's literature. Without thinking, she answered that yes, she was, she had taken a class in college. The man told her he thought she might be. He smiled at her, and she looked away from him.

The man came back to the gas station a few days later in a different car, an expensive one. Again he dawdled over the transaction, showing no interest in what he was saying. He watched her closely the entire time, she knew, gathering details. This time before he left he asked her another question. She had handed him the charge slip. He signed the slip, but held the plastic board close to him and looked up at her. He knew it sounded a bit awkward, he told her, but he was an artist, and he wondered if she would consider posing for him. He said he found her face terribly beautiful, and he would love to capture it in a photograph. He pulled a blue business card from his shirt pocket and gave it to her. The card bore only a name and a telephone number. She took the card and thanked him politely. She told him she wouldn't do it. She told him—she felt stupid about this now, that she hadn't been more direct—that she was not beautiful and would feel silly posing. The man laughed and told her that that was fine, but a shame, and would she please keep his card.

How did the man know when she worked? She knew that he had been watching her, or had asked questions of the other station attendants.

A week later the man came in again. She pictured him driving aimlessly about the city, trying to use up his gas. She had to wait on him. She was the only person working when he came in, a slow stretch late in the afternoon. She was quick with him now, as rude as possible, curt. When it came time for him to leave, his face seemed to brighten, suddenly animated. Handing her the signed charge slip, he told her that he had changed his mind about her posing for him. A photograph would never do, nor a painting. He called her by her name. She hated that. He wanted to sculpt her, a full figure. Could she come over Saturday, he wondered, and he would make a plaster mold of her. First the body and then the head. He would use that mold as a guide while she posed for him in the backyard in the natural light. You are so beautiful, he told her. She told him flatly that she would do no such thing and walked away and locked herself in the office and hid there for ten minutes. He was gone when she came out.

That day she asked the manager of the gas station to change her schedule. She told him that she wanted to take some classes that were beginning immediately.

She did not see that man again, but two weeks later she found an envelope taped to her locker at work. Her first name was written on the envelope. Inside was a green piece of paper, folded once. It was a map of a cemetery. Written at the top of the card was the message "I am here," with a line drawn from the message to a gravesite. The grave was her father's, where he'd been buried five years earlier. She walked behind the station, still holding the card, and cried for some minutes next to the garbage dumpster. She quit that afternoon.

The evening had come on full. I could see nothing more outside the windows. My friend got up and turned on the heater, which started with a thump. We sat together in the house, surrounded by the darkness now.

I asked her a question.

No, she told me, he hadn't hurt her.

Her husband came home a little while later, carrying their son asleep against his shoulder. They'd been at his grandmother's. The boy had had fun; he'd been spoiled and was up way past his bedtime. Maybe he'd sleep later the next morning.

"That'll be the day," she said.

She took her son from her husband and took him off to bed. Her husband seemed tired. I made him a drink, and we sat together in the living room. We could hear her talking to the child, hushing, comforting. She came back in and motioned us to follow her. She whispered.

"You guys, come here. You have to see him before I turn out the lights. He's so beautiful."

Five and Dime

You have to know how much I hate this. By the time I get to after-school, a little late, Sam's on the verge of tears. He's a big kid, nine, but why shouldn't he cry? And he's still my baby. It's raining, pouring, December dark, and after-school's been closed and locked for forty-five minutes. Sam knows that sometimes I'm late—it's happened before—but still. I called the school to let them know, and like every other time, they plead there's nothing they can do, they've got families, too, he'll have to wait outside. He'll be okay, they tell me.

Sam's huddled under the little porch by the school's multi-purpose room, afraid to move away from the cone of light there, afraid of the shadowy playground and the slick river of traffic beyond the fence. He's got his backpack on, it drags him down, he's ready to go. When he sees me, he bolts through the rain, his backpack bumping, he whispers Mom and runs right into my arms. I can feel the heat from his face, feel the sob rise up in his chest, then he sighs and the evening runs out of him, he collapses into me, uncurls. I hate this.

I have a pretty good deal at work, considering, but every so often there's some sales report that can't possibly wait, and I have to stay and tweak it, knowing full well the report will sit on Harmon's desk all the next day, probably over the weekend, too.

I mean, give me a break. Even when I get out on time, I don't get to Sam until six, and he's stuck in after-school, reading, drawing, waiting. I imagine him waiting there with the other kids, every once in a while looking out the window, wondering if he'll ever get out.

And tonight has to be a Thursday, our special night, though not much of one. We take the train back to our neighborhood and go straight to the Five and Dime, eat grilled cheese at the counter, chocolate milkshake for dessert. Sam always gets to pick out a little something for himself.

I ask Sam if he still wants to go, maybe it's too late or too cold, and there's that sob again, clouding behind his eyes. He nods and nods, whispers a thin yes, then sees something in my look, and there goes the sob, winding out of him. We head for the train.

❧

It's possible we moved into our neighborhood because of the Five and Dime. We'd been looking at apartments for days when we found this one, the one we're still in, a basement unit in the back, small and dark but nice enough, nice enough for Sam, little trooper, to call it rustic, a word I could not have imagined he'd know. I wanted to take the place immediately, out of sheer fatigue and hunger and a general pissiness that we had to do this at all, when Sam spotted the Five and Dime and its old-timey lunch counter and offered to buy me dinner. With his own money, his allowance. Now and then I have to remind myself that he's very sharp at reading other people, too good perhaps, too attentive.

Walking into Irving Variety Five and Dime was like stepping

into my own past, and the first thing that told me this was the smell of the place, popcorn and butter and salted nuts, a bit of tang from the grill, the slight mustiness of things that haven't been moved in a while. There'd been a store like this in San Jose when I was growing up, a Ben Franklin, and I'd stop there on the way home from school to buy candy or pencils, and sometimes with friends, in junior high mostly, we'd have lunch at the counter on weekends, feeling very grown-up. I bought my first bra there, without my mother knowing, ashamed to be buying it in such a store, not a department store, but relieved to be anonymous. The salesgirl wasn't much older than me, and she had bad skin and braces and seemed very unhappy, so it was perfect. The only time I ever tried to steal anything from anyone was from Ben Franklin, nail polish, Cherries in the Snow, but after walking around with it in my purse for a long time and pretending to be ruthlessly interested in every piece of merchandise in the store, I relented and put the polish back in its little rack, the end of my life of crime.

The day Sam and I first found Irving Variety was just like today, rainy and cold, the heart of winter's clipped days, two years ago now, and we both fell into the comfort of the place, the crowded aisles, the racks of cheap and cheerful and overlooked goods—tube socks, votive candles, ledgers, cookie cutters, jigsaw puzzles. I let Sam buy me dinner that first time. He was so proud of himself.

When we left that night, the little shopping street was all lit up, and we chased the shop windows in the rain, the shoemaker, the comics shop, the photo store, coin store, notary, a few cafés. We agreed to take the apartment, and I called the manager that night and wheedled and promised, and we got it. Paul had left us the year before and was living with his new girlfriend by then and she was already pregnant, so Sam and I had no choice but to move smaller. Paul and his new family could afford to move to Belvedere, in a big house that overlooked the bay and the city. With what I was making and the child support from Paul, Sam and I would just barely get by. That first year we were separated, Paul was super dad, taking Sam all the time and making promises to me about how good everything would turn out. Then Debbie showed up, and they were pregnant and moving into the big house, and Sam and I were suddenly out of our lovely flat, and Paul decided it was best for Sam to stay with me in the city for school. Sam knew all too well what it meant, he'd have the bedroom, I'd sleep on the couch, and so he allowed the quiet charm of this poky little neighborhood get to him. He made it appeal to him. All the merchants know Sam now, and if we miss a single Thursday night at Irving Variety's counter, they worry. We feel at home here.

℘

    The train comes up out of the tunnel into our neighborhood. The rain's stopped and the sky's practically clear. But colder, too, really cold. The shop windows are all steamed up. I feel the skin on my face pinch. If I know anything about the weather here, all this points to a week of very cold and dry weather when the rain stops, it happens every year around this time. The problem is, we're not ready for this weather, don't have the heavy coats and boots and gloves for the cold. This isn't Canada, after all. I'd prefer that it rain, swamp us, it's warmer that way.

Irving Variety is toasty inside, the ceiling heater blowing overtime. Dan and Treung, the owners, are behind the front counter, watching their small black and white, Wheel of Fortune, I think. They wave and call Sam over, offer him a toffee, a candy I know he doesn't like but which he dutifully accepts and pops in his mouth. He mumbles a thank you, and we all laugh a little. Like every Thursday.

Mrs. Park, cook and waitress, see us, smiles broadly, then turns and begins to make our sandwiches. She knows what we'll have, there's no need to order. We sit on our usual stools at the far end of the counter, where we can watch everything come and go, keep an eye on who's passing by. Usually Sam and I spend dinner talking about the other customers, invent surprising histories for them. That one may look like an old lady, Sam'll say, but in reality she's a spy in the service of the evil Dr. Xanadu, and Sam, secret agent that he is, will have to save me from her evil clutches.

Tonight Sam goes on and on about the California mission system, and I'm happy to let him, and he's happy to tell me. They're studying how Spanish priests and soldiers made their way north from Baja and established a chain of small settlements. In the beginning it must have been so hard for them, Sam tells me, but they knew that one day they would build great cities here. Just think, Mom, he says, how far away they must have felt, Spain was far away, and all they had here was adobe and grass.

Over our shakes, Sam is telling Mrs. Park about the missions. He'll talk anyone's ear off. Mrs. Park nods and smiles and says, You don't say, which is how she keeps him talking. Sam draws a map for her, in crayon on one of the paper place mats. This is California, right?, he says, and see, they put the missions here and here and here, each one of them a day's horse ride from the other. They didn't have very much back then, especially the riders out on their own. They could only carry what they could carry, just enough to get them to the next outpost. You don't say, Mrs. Park says.

Later, Sam's glued to the glass cabinet of roasted nuts, and who can blame him. You can see the rich oils sweating out of the nuts, smell the dark surprise brought out by the hot lights in the case. They're expensive, I know that and Sam knows that, but it's been such a shitty day, why not. I order a half pound of cashews. Mrs. Park gently scoops the nuts out of their bin and empties them into a white paper bag. She hands me a chit and I go up front to pay. Sam hangs back in the toy section.

At the register I hand over the chit, fish out my wallet, and pay, and that's it, there's not a single bill left in there. Two quarters, we're done. Paul's check was supposed to be here Monday, but it wasn't, and when I called he apologized and told me it was on its way and it probably is. But still. I do get paid tomorrow but that's tomorrow and not tonight, and I'm the one who wants to break into tears now, there's not enough for the smallest trinket. I could charge it, but you know how that works, and I just don't know how much more into debt we can go.

Sam's standing by the wire rack of toys at the back of the aisle. These are the toys Sam's used to getting from me. Plastic paratroopers, jacks, Chinese jump rope, small bags of Army men, a stack of play money, glitzy crowns. Sam hands me the bag of cashews—he's saved my portion for me—then wipes his salty fingers on his pants before he picks up what he's been staring at. We've looked at this before, and I know he's wanted to get it but has been waiting for the right moment. Magic Crystal Garden, five-forty-nine, in a box about so big by so big. The picture on the box shows a Japanese looking rock garden with two bonsai trees growing out of it and between these a miniature Mt. Fuji that's supposed to be in the distance. You soak a cardboard skeleton of the garden in the solution, and over the next hour, the trees bloom and Mt. Fuji turns all blue and snow-capped. I suppose there's some educational value here, something about the science of minerals, but mostly it's cool looking.

Listen. I know Sam will be fine without this gewgaw, that his life would go on unimpeded, unharmed. And besides, at his father's on alternate weekends, he has more toys than a hundred kids could want. This is not a big deal. But I want him to have it, I want to get it for him tonight.

He's reading the directions on the back of the box now, and this means he wants it, he's made his choice. Do you want it, Sam, I ask, and the sound of his name in the air, unnecessary and unexpected, slays me. Oh yes, he says, always so polite. I take the box from him, tell him to keep looking while I pay.

They are so good to us here, I hate to do it, but in the housewares aisle, surrounded by cheap dishes and flimsy towels, I slip Sam's present deep into the bottom of my purse. I'll pay for it somehow.

⁂

After he's done with his homework, Sam readies the Magic Crystal Garden. He covers the kitchen table with newspapers taped together, and fills a Tupperware container with water. He mixes the galvanizing solution into the water, and we wait the required five minutes. Wearing my yellow dish gloves, he then immerses the skeleton of the garden, and we wait another ten minutes, which Sam fills by poring over the instruction booklet to find out as much as he can about the formation of these rudimentary patterns. Sam loves this line he finds in the instructions, Please to avoid rude accelerations, and we laugh and laugh, and cannot figure it out for the life of us.

Finally it's ready, and Sam gently removes the garden from the solution and sets it on its base. It may take, according to the fine print, as nearly tall as two durable hours for full floweration. Sam's got an idea. He puts on a CD, The Beatles "Let It Be," his new favorite, then he grabs two storm candles from the kitchen, lights them and sets them on the kitchen table, and turns off all the lights. It's lovely. I turn up the heater a notch.

The Magic Crystal Garden begins to grow. On the black branches of the artificial trees, feathery shafts of matter begin to appear. Sam explains that it's magnetism of a sort, the crystal molecules aligning with one another, and in that alignment, parallel now, they accrue—he actually uses that word—and make new shapes where there's been nothing before. Mom, he says, it's simple, they push each other up.

The leaves of the tree are pink, the branches yellow, and the tiny flowers in the garden—not pictured on the box—are red and green. Mt. Fuji is the best, though. In the dim light of the storm candles it does seems far away, seems like a real mountain that's hazy and impossible to get to. You can almost see the unbroken trail of pilgrims winding their way, the ones who every day make their way to the top, for what? Is it heaven, they expect, nirvana? I love the view from here, the view of that distant mountain.

The Weather Tomorrow

The traffic was stalled on the bridge, everyone getting away early, the bay already filled with the white flags of sailboats. The weather was going to be perfect, all the reports said so—temperatures were soaring, a little smoggy, but generally hot and clear, a classic California weekend. Ted was happy, no, nearly delirious there above the Golden Gate with the weekend stretched out ahead of him. This was near the end of summer, on the verge of autumn, a few high feathery clouds, the stereo turned way up. For the first time in ages, Ted's dance card was full, five official engagements.

It started tonight with a very French dinner party at the Chases in Marin, up Cabin Road, then Saturday, down the coast to Aptos for the annual B-B-Q in the boss's apple orchard, always a blowout. He'd leave there early, at three or four, say, and head back north to Millbrae for Mai Tai madness with a bunch of the gang from Capp, and then Sunday there was KT's wedding, his second, at Rollie's vineyard in St. Helena, followed that night in the city with a quiet cocktail party put on by one of his clients. Sitting on the bridge, Ted imagined all the new people he might meet and what he might tell them about the new position.

Ted had moved out of the house in late May and hadn't done much of anything except work all summer, but things were looking up at work, definitely, the new position and all, and he was feeling energized and ready to get out again. Sure, he might run into Triss at Rollie's wedding, which he did not want to do, but if he did he could handle it, and she might have Katie with her. He missed his stepdaughter. Who knew?

$$e$$

Chris and Alicia Chase had hired a caterer for a four-course gourmet meal in celebration of their eleventh anniversary. Yes, it was expensive, but nothing like last year; that was something, even Triss had a good time. Given all that had happened to them since, the Chases were feeling quieter. They had admittedly invited Ted as sort of a set-up with Lucia from Alicia's work, no pressure though, all very nice of them but also weird because Alicia was Triss's friend.

Everyone stood on the deck in the near evening and drank expensive wine while the young catering couple worked in the exposed kitchen, mincing and saucing, reducing, clarifying. The house was set on the eastern slope of the last mountain before Stinson Beach, above a close valley of scrub oak and manzanita.

"I don't care about subtleties, this is not weather I tell you," Stan was saying. "It's beautiful but it's not weather. Philly is weather. This is scenery."

Ted leaned against the railing and watched the hushed green of the hillside give way to panged orange. This color of light was its own season to him.

"No," he told Stan. "Any fool can tell the difference between eight feet of snow and ninety-nine degree summer. Here, it's something you smell, the change of season. We're about ten minutes from fall right now. It smells like cabernet."

Ted was the only native at the party. Stan and Carole were two months out of Philly, Carlo and Jessie had transferred here from Houston two years before, Lucia came out for school from Boston and stayed, and the Chases, originally from Long Island, had been here almost twenty years but still complained to know nothing of the weather.

Lucia had moved away from the group and was flushed with late sun, her arms and legs luminous with hair.

"It's all backwards here," Ted told them. "Summer is winter, everything dead and pulled back. There's no rain, and the hills lose their color and some days it's almost all white, migraine white. But winter, when the rains come back, late November maybe, everything starts to grow again, and then it's green. The plum trees blossom in February."

"It's too easy, that's what matters," Stan said. He was jabbing at Ted with his merlot. "It's too easy here. No hardships; no character. A little snow would work wonders I'm telling you."

"You know," Carole said. "It's the sky. Back east, the sky isn't nearly so big. The first time I saw it here, I cried. I still get dizzy from it."

At dinner Ted wanted to tell everybody about the promotion, but it never seemed to fit in at the right place. He had rehearsed what he would say, and it had sounded good when he was stuck in traffic on the bridge with all the boats at play below him, but at dinner, seated across from Lucia, the caterers fluttering, and Stan pretty much hogging it all, the new position seemed too difficult to explain with any real weight. It *was* a big break for him, that was certain, but to detail it, how he would be in the office two days a week now, moving off the road, bigger accounts; no, no new title, but a vote of confidence. He had all weekend to talk about it.

So they talked about the weather across the artichoke salad, shrimp cocktail, duck breast with grilled squashes, scallops in lime juice, and the dessert, which the caterers comped because they were friends too, the harvest-apple espresso apricot sorbets. So much of everything.

Ted didn't really get a good look at the catering couple until he tromped through the kitchen where the woman was doing dishes and stowing the rented glassware. He washed his hands at the kitchen sink only to watch her for a moment: dark, meticulous, lush.

When he got back to the table, Lucia had already left. She wanted Ted to know that she really enjoyed meeting him, but she had an early day tomorrow, hoped he'd understand, and looked forward to seeing him again.

Later, the moon from the deck was Ted's favorite moon of all, gibbous, just past full, those three or four days where it's huge and bright, especially this time of year, and slowly waning.

Alicia asks as Ted's leaving, "By the way, how are you, are you okay?"

ex

The B-B-Q was subdued this year, no talent show, no band. Eating and drinking in the orchard. The company had posted another stellar year, five straight, and owned some share of prestige for a paper place, order forms, triplicates, receipt books, an oddly hip place, a good place to work, and in the first few years the abundance of these B-B-Qs dazzled, but last year, and even more so this year, everyone was a little fried by the enthusiasm. Let's be honest, they worked you like dogs. But as Ted often said, a bit conspiratorially, jeez, what money *wasn't* he making. Huge.

He yakked it up with everybody, but he saw these people all the time, and something about the day and the green painted picnic benches made him want to step aside, so he wandered through the gridded, lacy orchard to the nearest hill, and found a eucalyptus grove, a long dirt road hollowed by windbreaks.

When Ted's in transit, making the deals city by city, he often follows back roads for the peace of them, and several times he's come across groves much like this, and stopped there. He thinks he remembers such a place—he's eight or nine—just like this though, the sun high but falling, and he can never quite name it. In the hot shade, the listless dust and eucalyptus braided with the distant cooking smells, and suddenly he knew. A picnic—a work picnic!—with his father, and it's late in the afternoon, he's been swimming all day, and he's ravenous for steak.

Ted leaned against an old bit of fence and tried to remember more until Jennifer came up and caught him smoking one of the cigarettes he'd fished out of the glove compartment. They hadn't seen each other in a while, and she thought he'd quit. She'd brought along a bottle of chardonnay and two glasses.

"So," she wanted to know. "You seen The Breasts lately?" Her nickname for Triss.

"Only her lawyer's breasts."

"Fuck, Ted, aren't you guys done yet?"

"No," he said. "Get back to me at half past forever."

"So listen," she said. "I always wanted to ask you, what do

they feel like? Are they perfect?"

"I hate them," he said. "I always hated them. It was her idea. They're naugahyde. Really. She feels upholstered."

"You paid for them."

"She told me she'd stay," he said. "A lovely parting gift instead."

Walking along, their shoulders touched, and then their flanks, and at one point, Ted even put his arm around her. The grove was a safe place for them. When he tried to light a second cigarette, Jennifer snatched it from his mouth and crushed it. Every once in a while, they caught slivers of the bay, perfectly blue, and the feathery clouds.

"You know," she said calmly, stopping. "You're fucked. I don't even get it. I mean. You flirt, but no. Then you're getting divorced, so we sleep together, and then you actually do fucking leave her and that's the end of us. I hear nothing from you. You're just stupid. I had to tell you that."

She looked at him earnestly and headed back to the B-B-Q. From the far end of the grove, she turned to him.

"I mean, how could you marry someone you met at the Super Bowl?"

With the day behind her, through the sheer dress, Jennifer's body was clear to him.

Ted drank the last of the chardonnay and smoked the last of the cigarettes while the grove lengthened, deepened, and grew still hotter.

꒰

Mai-Tai Madness had been a bad idea to start with. Most of the gang had been out all day at other parties and were already pretty wasted by the time they got to George's Place, their favorite bar since high school when George himself ran the place and looked the other way. They'd been having Mai-Tai Madness every year forever, and frankly, as they snuck up on forty, and while most of them still showed up, there was more fun in the promise of it. To top it off, Ted got stuck on the summit in mammoth traffic, slow and sweaty, so he'd stopped off at the apartment to shower, and it was way past dark and everyone was already trashed and roaring when he cruised into George's.

Dean and Allan conspired at the bar, and Ted knew right away they'd been snorting. He didn't feel up to that right now, so he drank Mai-Tais as fast as he could, hoping to catch up even though that seemed impossible.

Dean, as always, was talking about sex. He was telling them about a stripper he'd been seeing on the side, and what she could do, and how paying for it was really worth it, cheaper in the long run. Allan and Ted were both nodding and laughing. Would he ever change?

"The weird thing," Dean said, "is that when I'm fucking some other thing, Cookie gets all hot again, and starts dressing right, and all she wants to do is lose the kids and suck all night. Hidden assets. But Ted-O, hey man, you're free again. Free and loose and riding the big road and, man, that's gotta be the life. If it weren't for the kids."

Ted leaned in and yelled over the music, the same songs they'd listened to for twenty years, *This is not my beautiful house*, a dance favorite.

"That's what I wanted to tell you," he was telling the both of them. "I got sort of a promotion. See, I'll be in the office two days a week, slowly getting off the road. It's a big deal."

"Not the office," Allan said. "You're doomed."

"Hey, cool," Dean said. "But look, my pager's beeping. Ah, yes, the snowman calleth, and you know it tolls for thee. Gentleman, assume the positions."

In the bathroom, crammed into one stall, they snorted off a matchbook cover. Ted demurred at first, but one look from Dean killed that, and the next thing he knew he was three lines up.

"No-no-no-no-no-no-no-body's fault but mine," Dean howled. "I feel like dancing."

Ted was trying to talk to Allan about Dean, about how all he wanted to say to Dean was no, don't do these things, no, but Allan was just nodding and smiling, and then Mindy came up, shot a faux smile at Ted, took Allan's hand and melted into the crowd.

Mindy still looked good, better really, especially dancing, and maybe he should have taken her up on it two years ago, the night she'd cornered him in the garage at some party and kissed him, maybe he should have started something there, left Triss, or never lied about how much money he had and married Triss in the first place, or certainly not paid for her boobs, maybe none of it, but that was stupid because he knew that there was only this night, this weekend, and that's what mattered, didn't it, that's what all this time was about, so he'd just better forget all the dachshunds yipping in his head, it was just the drugs anyway. He should have known better. What was he, some college boy?

If it wasn't so late he would have called Katie. She was twelve years-old and adored making fun of the stupid things adults did.

They could have had a good laugh.

He danced into the crowd with his Mai-Tai, to shake off some of the jag, dancing up to a spot near Mindy, but she wouldn't even look at him. They were all yelling, laughing, dancing, and drinking—*Same as it ever was*—but none of it helped, the dachshunds were still yapping, so Ted bummed a cigarette from Cookie and went out into the hot night and watched the swift parade of bright cars on the El Camino, the buzzing neon and the jets lumbering into the air. A night like this was so rare along the bay, shirt sleeves weather at midnight, maybe eight times a year, and he was glad to be out in it. No, he was telling Dean, no, just no, just that, don't.

He bought a pack of cigarettes at Palmieri Liquors, and headed up the hill to his apartment, where he watched the airport below him until four in the morning. This was why he'd rented this particular apartment, for a night like this, the moon's insistent light.

❧

The caterers had set up the bar under the wide eaves of the old shipping barn, along with the cake and gift table, the deejay and the dance floor. The dinner tables were scattered in among a loose section of old vines near the edge of the rolling green and gold vineyards. All of the tables were dressed in white with gold and burgundy overlays. Ted had arrived just as the wedding procession left for the olive grove near the river bottom where the ceremony was to be held. Still time for a Bloody Mary.

"Big do?" he asked the bartender.

"A hundred and seventeen, not including kids. Do-able."

The bartender hit Ted again, and lit up a cigarette himself while they watched KT and Gigi, second marriage for both, wind down the dusty truck road. There they were, in black and white again, surrounded by their friends and family in all their peacock colors. Ted was fairly certain Triss was not among the crowd.

"My buddy from college," he was telling the bartender, who was suddenly friendly. "Rollie, too. We all met there on the same dorm floor. This is Rollie's place, and Sally's; he won it from his family in a lawsuit. Don't even talk about KT's first marriage, it's been justifiably shrouded in silence. I think this one though, yeah, I think this one might possibly could work."

Far north in the valley, Mt. St. Helena stood rather grimly over it all, barren and angular, as if some shadow were cast on it from the clearest of hot, blue skies, as if the mountain were already in autumn while the rest of the narrow valley baked in summer. Dusky, that was it, that must be the word. Dusky and stern.

Ted had one more drink and one more cigarette and ran down the path to reach the party just as the ceremony began. There was something appropriate, almost official, about Ted running down late with his sunglasses and drink, and both KT and Rollie looked around at the last second, a little toast between them. Ted stood at the edge of the grove, leaning against an olive tree for shade, and closely watched the crowd gather and quiet. During the ceremony he closed his eyes, and for just a second, he could almost fall to sleep in the ripe air.

$\backsim$

Triss arrived even later than Ted. Horribly late. Dinner had already been served. Ted knew that Triss hadn't been invited, but he suspected that she might show up here because the woman was insane over being left out, and of all the parties she'd been left out of this weekend, the wedding was the one that would make her most insane. It didn't matter if it was KT's wedding. She barely tolerated KT, and had told Ted so the first night she met him, but Ted could almost hear her saying to Gigi, "We just *had* to come, it's so important to us." So, she just showed her insecure little ass up, dragging Katie behind her.

Katie looked so different, in only two months, she was much taller. She was wearing a pale blue dress with orange birds on it, a long slinky dress, sleeveless, with chunky platform shoes. Her hair was changed, too, parted in the middle. The last time he'd seen her, Katie was wearing black sweatpants and one of Ted's t-shirts. When she and her mom stopped to look over the crowd, Katie cocked her hip and stared out past the vineyards, running a finger back and forth on the inside of her necklace chain. Ted couldn't tell if she wanted to seem sexy or bored, or if she was embarrassed by her mom at this wedding or embarrassed by her mom in general.

Ted looked right at Triss, to make sure, and she did see him, but for once acted with some decency, joining a half empty table on the far side of the party.

Triss threw down her purse and nearly ran over to KT and Gigi at the head table, where she made a big show of giving them their gift, an enormous box wrapped in Mylar, saying much too much about it, and kissing the both of them. Katie would have none of this, and had already gone to the buffet tables on the barn porch where she made a plate for herself and a plate for her mom. She saw Ted, smiled, started to set down the plates, then shrugged and pointed with her head to Triss who was still cooing. Then Katie shot him a big, old goofy face and Ted nearly spit out his wine.

"No," Ted was telling Sally and Rollie. "Our lawyers talk now. If I need something from the house, Triss makes sure Katie's gone when I show, and the door's always left wide open so I don't even have to knock. It's better this way. Easier for everybody I think."

"You should at least dance with her," Sally said. "Katie I mean. Look, she's all dressed up to dance, and there's nobody here but you to do that. Look at her dress."

"She'd be too embarrassed."

"Don't be stupid," Rollie said. "At least she'd be embarrassed by something worthwhile."

"You're right," Ted said. "It's no big deal. Triss has had the odd moment of clarity. You never know."

After the cake was served, Rollie, KT, and Ted stood far away from the crowd, drinking some of KT's best out of real crystal. The sun was lowering, the shadows were long, and the late summer dust reddened around them.

"Here we go again," Rollie said, toasting KT.

"Amen," KT said. "Amen. Can't get lucky enough. And by the way, divorce, I know for a fact, Monsieur Chucklehead, is no reason to take up smoking again."

"Relapse," Ted said, lifting his glass.

The deejay called KT to the dance floor, where he and Gigi got it all going, and when they'd worked through all the parents, and Rollie and Sally, Ted went over to the table where Triss and

Katie sat alone.

"Hello, Triss," Ted said as calmly as he could. "Hey, Katie." He wanted to put his hand on Katie's head, stroke her hair once lightly. "Look, I don't want it to be too awkward, but would you mind if I danced with Katie. That is, if she wants to."

There must have been something between Ted and Triss once, but Triss looked so tired now, or maybe it was just the heat of the day, the long drive, the late start.

"Sure," Triss said. She sort of smiled. "That'd be fine. Maybe she'd stop moping and I could actually have a good time."

Katie was suddenly sitting up straight, her hands clasped in her lap, playing anxious.

"Young lady," Ted said, bowing, extending his hand. "If I may have the pleasure and edification of this dance, I humbly pray you."

"Why, kind sir," Katie said. She rose on Ted's hand, and curtsied. "The honor is all mine. Mother, send the coach at midnight, be a dear."

On the dance floor, Ted presented Katie, then held his arms out stiffly from his body, as if at a beginner's dance lesson, and he and Katie twirled slowly around the floor to The Stones.

"Guess what," Katie was saying. "Mom says I can take surfing lessons."

"No way."

"Yeah, when we go back..."

"Back where?"

"Yeah," Katie said. "You know, like when we get back to the house tonight, and maybe tomorrow I can look around about surfing lessons."

"Oh," Ted said.

"I mean, you know," Katie said. "Look behind you. That woman should never ever wear that dress. We may have to write her up."

They danced every single song, sometimes their stately waltz, sometimes the tribal boogie, and once, Katie danced standing on Ted's feet. She was as light as a child, he was happy to discover.

"So, Katie-Potatie, tell me do," he said. "When you *do* go back to L.A., why do you want to take surfing lessons?"

"Because it's dangerous *and* beautiful," she said.

"Why do you want to do it if it's dangerous?"

"It's dangerous *and* beautiful, and I don't care if I get swept out to sea and I'm never heard from again. It'll still be beautiful."

℮

Triss had a long drive back, tons to do, so Katie kissed Ted on the cheek and gave him a big hug. They made their goodbyes.

While the caterers were cleaning up, Rollie and Ted wandered in the near vineyard. The harvest was almost here, Rollie said, and it was going to be a strong one, just the right amount of rain and heat, the proper level of sugars. Three years from now they'd have some damn fine wine. The sun was just setting behind the last low ridge, and the sky glowed vermilion, star dotted.

If Ted left right now, he could still make it to the last of the cocktail party. By waiting so long, he'd missed most of the bridge traffic and could pretty much glide into the city. He was tired, and part of him wanted to go straight home, but that would be a mistake, he knew, because Baker, one of his most important clients, should be expecting him, and besides, Baker understood the intricacies of the whole business, a guy Ted could talk to, and he'd know exactly how meaningful Ted's new position was, his prospects. Ted had not been to Baker's place before but had heard, over many a lunch, of the deck's swell view, the unsurpassable stretch of the Golden Gate and the bay as far as Mt. Diablo. Ted and Baker will stand on the balcony together and watch for signs of fog, follow the circling beacon of Alcatraz. They will discuss the delicacies of his move, what each little step forward means, yes, his prospects.

The drive across the bridge, windows wide open, clearly woke Ted up. The moon was rising by then, ebbed and beautiful.

Gravity

Newton is slow. Florence Chin has known this about her oldest son from the moment he was born. She may have even known it before, a sense of sluggish contentment that had flooded her then, but which she simply thought of as peace, one of many mysterious emotions that accompanied her pregnancy. In the first light of the birth, when Florence was able to look calmly at Newton—she and Xan had picked the name months in advance, certain the child would be a boy—she knew that something was wrong, although not terribly wrong. She said nothing at the time, certainly never mentioned her intuition to Xan. Instead Florence waited for a doctor to say the words, command in the air what she already knew in her body, and when Newton was six months old, a doctor did say them. There had been a problem, the doctor said, somewhere along the line, a lack of oxygen or crucial nutrition, and this had had an adverse effect on their son. No, he was not retarded, per se, the doctor would never say that—no one would ever say that—but Newton was going to be different, he would be slower than other children. Still, he should be healthy in most ways, and live an otherwise normal life.

Other doctors over the next three years confirmed this diagnosis, until at last, both Florence and Xan became inured to these conversations and their terms. Florence found great solace in the gossamer of words the doctors spun, the thin sentences stretched across the spaces of the unsayable. Wrapped in this thin coat Florence could forget the cigarettes and martinis that were her habit when she was pregnant with Newton, the cigarettes and martinis that had connected her to the earth then, had kept her stationed at the window of their flat during the long months, that had kept her, if only just, from drifting away. What had once been a difficulty, a situation—that slowness—became their lives. The doctors were right. Newton was slow, but otherwise okay.

Her younger son, Lee, was everything slow was not, especially these days. He had always been speed, crashing movement, quick jerks. Florence felt little of Lee during that pregnancy, so occupied with Newton and finding the words to say what they all knew. Lee was a skinny baby, not underweight, but thin in the arms and legs, his limbs strung as if on rubber bands. He walked at ten months, immediately began to run, and hasn't stopped since. When she says his name aloud, she sees him crossing a room, his body leaning into the air, falling to where it will go. Lee is two years younger than Newton, but as an infant passed him by and has remained the big brother.

But Newton, for all his slowness, is not heavy. You would think he is heavy, but he is not. He is slow, Florence has known for so long, precisely because he is light, weightless. When Florence tries to recall the exact moment she came to this knowledge, she can almost grasp it.

The boys were little, but who's to say exactly how old, somewhere between talking and going to school. They've always lived in this apartment—Xan insists on calling it a flat—which helps stir the memory. There, in the living room it must have been, and it seems to Florence that it's a torpid hour, eleven in the morning, say, and the sun is muted, too, hushed by the fog, so probably late summer. Florence has no idea where she stood in the scene, she sees only the old sofa and its geometrical print, the orange carpeting, the boys running around the glass-topped coffee table, and behind it all, the darkness of the rest of their rooms. She might have been standing anywhere; the image might as well come from a stranger's camera as from Florence's memory. When she begins to assemble this memory, as she sometimes does consciously, or when the image unexpectedly intrudes, what is most clear to her is the emotion that accompanied her realization, an emotion that has not dulled. She remembers the amazement of that moment, and that amazement is tied to a gratifying swell of sadness that brings tears to her eyes and which makes her want to laugh: the moment she realized Newton was not heavy.

She had always assumed he was heavy because he was slow— didn't those qualities go together? He was a big kid, chubby as a baby and never growing out of it, not even in puberty, which had stretched and twisted Lee a hundred ways. So Florence always assumed—he was slow because he was heavy. But on that day—at least her memory tells her this—when she saw her other son, Lee, racing away from his brother, and saw, when he turned sharply and cut back against the momentum of the chase, changing direction in an instant, she realized then what she still thinks of as an essential truth in her life: the slow are weightless. The quick in this world are not so because of their lightness, they are quick because they have gravity for traction, because they are heavy enough to gain a purchase on the earth and push off of it and through the air. The quick are so because of their weight. And Newton—poor

Newton, she'd say, but only to herself, only ever—poor Newton was slow precisely because he was weightless. He was a feather attempting to swim through the dull water of the world.

e

Now Newton had a job. He worked at the Coronet theater, down on Geary, a theater some called the Star Wars theater because it was one of the last single-screen theaters in the city and every special effects blockbuster opened there. The Coronet held some two thousand people, the loge was vast, the aisles wide, and an array of curtains opened and closed before every performance. On either side of the screen were bas-relief scenes, plaster painted gold, of two young noblemen, one bowing before his queen, the other lowering the crown, her coronet, upon her head. Florence loved these scenes, but not in a girlish way, rather in a serious, self-reflective way. Sitting in the near dark, waiting for a film to start, Florence would admire the queen and her attendants—of course she thought of them as herself and her two sons, for no other reason than the obvious—and she would wonder at the secrecy of this notion, how no one in the world would ever say, ah, yah, Florence, she really loves those bas-reliefs. Who would ever say such a thing?

Although the Coronet had been in San Francisco her entire life, Florence could not remember seeing a movie there until the children were born. She would go to the Coronet when she could find a sitter, and later, after school had started, always by herself, she'd go to get away from the close air of the empty flat.

Newton worked at the concession stand. No, Mom, he'd say,

it's not a candy counter, it's a concession stand, it's not a snack bar. Concessions, he'd say, with deliberation, with great practice. He also swept, vacuumed, and mopped, and one day, he told Florence, he hoped to work the ticket booth.

It was a perfect job for Newton. He had gone through school with great ease, much more easily than Lee had, and he'd enjoyed it, made friends in his own track, even once had a girlfriend who was also special—the word that had, over the years, replaced slow—and he'd graduated. For the next few years no one knew what to do for Newton. He took some crafts classes, but they had bored him. Until a few months before when Xan came home and announced that he'd found a job for his oldest son. There was such pride in his voice that day—both his sons were now working. A business acquaintance of Xan's—he had no friends, Florence thought, only business acquaintances—oversaw operations at the Coronet, and he always liked to hire a few special employees. Of course you do, Florence thought that night, knowing she was thinking a black thought, they never ask for more.

Lee had graduated the year after Newton, but he'd been working since he started high school. He worked at a tropical fish store, Fairy Lake Discus Palace. The father of Lee's best friend Charles owned the store, and Lee had joined on, at first cleaning tanks and such. A few years back, and Florence could not quite figure how this worked, Lee and Charles arranged to buy the store from Charles's father, every month getting closer to complete ownership. Lee continued to work hard at his studies, but college was out of the question. Who needs college to be in business, Xan would say? To run a business, you run a business, look at me, I didn't have to go to college to know that people need stove hoods, Lee is a smart boy.

Fairy Lake Discus Palace was, Lee often said with a pride as annoying as his father's, the second largest tropical fish emporium in the city—for the moment, he'd always add, wagging a finger. Where did the name come from, what did it mean? Only some fake Chinese bullshit, you know, Ma, to fool people. PR, marketing. In the heart of Clement Street, Chinatown's western suburb. Makes us sound spooky and old, doesn't it?

The shop was two floors of fish, every square inch filled with tanks and pumps and rock and splashing water. Yes, your typical fish, goldfish and carp and koi, angel and clown fish, fighting fish, neon tetras, hermit crabs. Lee and Charles, however, had recognized that this was the standard fare, and to distinguish their store, had begun to import rarer creatures, what Lee called exotica. Squid, octopi, jellyfish, seahorse, spiny-legged shrimp in blue and red shells, deadly puffer, and dead-looking rock fish. Expensive fish, fragile, with a high, per-item mark up.

Newton loved the fish and spent long hours at Fairy Lake Discus Palace. The only thing Florence did not like about the store was the music, loud boy music, drecky pop, booming through the store. Charles and Lee hired their friends, and the music they played was the sound testosterone would make if you could capture it. On a couple of occasions Florence had gone with Newton and Lee early in the morning, before the store was open. The quiet gurgle and hum of the tanks was transporting. At such times Florence thought she knew why it was called by such a strange name, Fairy Lake Discus Palace. At such times she felt as if she were inside one fish tank rather than surrounded by so many smaller ones.

Funny, Lee couldn't care less. It was simply a business to him, a good business. Where didn't you go in their world that didn't have an aquarium—dentist, restaurant, salon, home? Lee had always been a good brother to Newton, watching over him, had made his life as a special student easier and safer. There'd been a number of incidents when Lee was reprimanded by the schools for his protection of Newton; Florence never once seconded these punishments. He was a good brother. And Lee would spend time with him, tending to and admiring the fish. The aquarium in Newton's room was fifty gallons, tropical, salt water, and Lee made sure it was immaculate. Her sons spent what time they spent together these days in front of the fish tank, discussing the new species that had been added.

Most of the time the flat was empty. Xan was always gone, and Lee, too, and god knows where. Newton was at the Coronet.

❧

The martinis and cigarettes had come back. Not that Florence hadn't had a drink in all those years, nor the odd cigarette, but nothing like this ritual, which was to her simple and invariable. Every afternoon, she made and drank two martinis, starting at three, and while she drank them at the living room window of the flat, and overlooking nothing but the street and the opposing houses, with the tree line of the Presidio behind, she smoked four cigarettes, two with each drink. This took one hour. The ritual was exactly as it was when she was pregnant with Newton.

What she thought about then, well, that wasn't the question. She thought about nothing in particular, but it would not do to say she thought about *nothing*, nor that she was thoughtless, oblivious. Their flat was considered modern when they'd first bought it, that is, devoid of any reference to past architecture, certainly devoid of any hint of San Francisco's brief history of wooden Victorians and their cliché deep, bayed windows. To adhere to its modernity, then, the flat was flavorless, a series of cleanly rectangular rooms attached to one another, all arranged within an equally featureless exterior, all corners. The one surprise in the flat's scheme, and the only reason Florence had agreed to Xan's wish to buy it, were the windows that faced the street, floor to ceiling windows that made the day part of the flat. It wasn't that the view was better because of the windows, nor more capacious—did people who wore large spectacles see more than those who wore tiny frames?—it was that the wide and tall windows put you in the scene, drew you up into the view, and because the flat was on the top floor, the third floor, you stood in the air, hovering. Drinking her two martinis and smoking her four cigarettes, Florence Chin—she thought of herself that way, one word, her taken name—did not think, or not-think, while she looked out her window. She was drawn into the view, and for a while, alone, lived there in the air.

Around four Florence went into the dark kitchen, turned on the bright lights, and under a stainless stove hood—this is important, the hood was Xan's—she began to make dinner for her family. They would eventually come home.

It was simple enough to explain why the martinis and cigarettes had come back. The ritual had commenced with only a little thought and a trip to Park Liquors the week after Newton started at the Coronet. After twenty years. She moved her lunch dates and salon appointments forward, or rushed off from them with busy shrugs, and got herself home by three. Simple enough. Newton was at work now, and she was lonelier, that must be it, and while she'd stopped waiting for Lee and Xan years ago—one of them was always late, from the time Lee was nine—she could now wait for Newton, though most days he wouldn't come home until midnight. So, if asked, she would have said, yes, Newton, I'm lonely without him.

That was not the real reason, she knew, and later time told. It was Lee actually. With Newton gone more, her mind had turned to Lee, and what she knew and suspected of his life, that now occupied her, surprisingly so, and she was anxious all the time, and so her ritual. All this was confirmed the day the police came to the door.

It was during her ritual, halfway through the first martini, when Florence would normally have ignored the buzzer, but there was a quality to the sound that was enervating, as if there were a short in the wiring.

The young officer seemed surprised by the martini glass in her hand. He was a sweet-looking boy, scrubbed, bland, someone Lee might have been if he hadn't been himself. Foolishly, she offered him a drink. She was terrified. He pulled out a small pad of paper, and it seemed to flip open on its own. The smile leaked from officer Lum.

Did she know a Leonard X. Chin, and was he a resident here, and if so, was he home at the moment? Was her son the registered owner of a 2001 Honda Civic, lilac in color, two Robert Henry

Victor eight nine one? Was the car kept at this address? Did she know where her son might be found?

The lilac Civic, Lee's sole purpose, the reason he seemed so intent on making the business work. Prum-brossom, that's how he described the color, that's funny, Ma. Never serious. Lee spent every moment in the car, as though work and home were the transits between his real life. Tricked out, top to bottom, small but powerful. An immaculate paint job, impossible stereo, tinted windows. Like all the other boys, Lee had installed neon runners to the bottom of the chassis, and as he drove along, the car seemed to float above the asphalt. Florence had seen him from half a mile away at night on Geary. Xan had purchased the Honda as a gift, but Lee had made and paid for all the modifications, all total about forty-five thousand.

It seemed that the car had been involved in an altercation last Thursday. No, there had not been an accident. A citizen had filed a report. The driver of the car, the report said, had followed a pedestrian and attacked him after a brief shouting match at an intersection. He managed to get the license number, described the assailant as a young Asian man. Did Florence have any knowledge of the situation?

Last Saturday. What could she remember? Lee had come home from work, gone into his room, vanished again. She saw him sometime Sunday afternoon, they'd all had dinner at home. She was supposed to have noticed something. She told officer Lum what she knew. Lee would be at Fairy Lake Discus Palace.

This is why the cigarettes and martinis had come back, she knew now, she had been waiting for this, for Lee's trouble. It was bound to happen, she'd been carrying the knowledge of it for years. Too much money, his cock-hipped swagger, the sleek polish of the car, the jagged laughter of his friends. Whenever she went to the store, a sudden decorum swept over the boys, Lee suddenly solicitous, as if a deal had just transpired and piles of cash littered the floor. The halos of sinners in church. In the back of the store, the ancestors' shrine, red and gold, fake candles, but real sacrifices—sesame balls, rice, beer, oil. Warding off which evil spirits?

She was certain that most of it—it, Lee's dubious life—was small-time, petty, inconsequential. He was a thug, that's all, just like his father.

e⁓

Lee denied everything, though not very well. He came home early, around six, knowing full well he would be alone with his mother. Newton would be at the Coronet until midnight, and Xan, well, Xan was out wherever it was Xan went out to—Florence suspected the worst of where he might be, but she covered this up, always had, with an image of Xan driving around the city in his big gold Mercedes, driving, alone and arrogant, through the canyons of the city he considered his empire, a city of stove hoods. Lee had come home with a purpose, to try out his story.

Ma, he said, and very casually gave her a hug, his first mistake. Florence reheated their dinner, and they ate in the kitchen, at the breakfast bar. The fog was already in, thick but high, and the evening was warm, dark, snug. Lee began with contrition.

Ma, he said, did a policeman come here today?

If he'd been in the right, he'd have attacked. What did she tell that policeman?

She told him what she knew, told him she was waiting for an answer.

It's funny, he said. I loaned my car to Toy, and he says he argued with this guy, sure, but he never attacked him or anything. Up on Stanyan, by Real Foods. Nothing happened, but you know Toy, he's got a mouth.

• Florence was eating. A young Asian male, so simple, jeans and t-shirt, dark jacket, sunglasses. Even she can't tell them apart.

Did Toy attack this man?

No, Lee said, eating finally, but he should have, you know, because this guy actually hit my car, slapped it with his hand, bam, real loud, could have done real damage, you know. You shouldn't hit other people's property, that simple, I mean an argument's an argument, that simple. You hit you get hit. Simple. But Toy would never do that, he's a chicken. And the car's okay.

No, Lee said, no, no one was hurt.

Fine, Florence told him. It'll be okay. I'll talk to your father, then you talk to him, just to be safe. Nothing will happen. Your father will talk to Ben, just in case. Now, don't be stupid. You drive your car.

How odd for that man, what a strange twist in his day. Not the argument, that was life in the city. Lee always drove too fast, cutting corners, and the man almost gets killed, and without thinking, he hits the car, slap, on the roof, plum blossom roof, bam, slap, bark. Stop that. They yell, he moves on. The man is walking down the street, going home probably, or to a friend's, putting the story together in his head, to tell everyone and get rid of the story—he almost killed me—staring up at the fog-dead sky, just walking. It was foggy on Saturday, had been for weeks, the thick of it.

Then there is a flapping motion around his shoulders. How odd, the man thinks in the first fraction of the moment—the whole thing lasts five, ten seconds, a flash—how odd, I'm being attacked by a bird, a very large bird, a hawk perhaps, but why? Then in the next sliver of time, it becomes apparent it's no bird, but another person, fists, chest against back, the fists are wild and inconclusive, and the man thinks, okay, I'm being beaten up, but who could it possibly be and why are they doing this to me, and that sliver of time clicks to the next, and the man knows who it is, that punk in the purple Civic, of course, who else, and now the man, his shoulders hunched, hands near his face, is being pushed down to his knees and into a corner of a house, where the garage door is inset. By now he's gathering himself, can sense he is bigger than this punk, and he's starting to turn, rising and turning, he's going to hit back, but Lee has turned, all gravity and traction, spun and fled, and by the time the man recovers, Lee is halfway down the block, and then he cuts the next corner, pling, gone down that way, and gone again no doubt. There, right across the street, the Civic, the same one, not purple really, lighter than that, the color intense, glowing in the high, warm fog, lilac. The man takes out a piece of paper and a pen, and writes down all the information.

c⌒

Xan came home at ten, had already eaten, and Florence told

him what she knew, then sent him to Lee's room. Xan would berate Lee for this, but in a most irritating fashion, would manage to show his pride in his son—see, Lee is tough, Lee is shrewd.

Just after eleven, Florence rose from the couch and the television. Xan and Lee were still talking, murmuring, all business. Newton often took the bus home, 38 Geary, practically a straight shot, but sometimes Florence went to pick him up. When she couldn't sleep, provoked by an imaginary concern—he'd be robbed, teased, get lost— she would show up at the theater early, and sit in the lobby and watch Newton work, comforted by this, and yes, full of pride. On the way to the Coronet she passed Fairy Lake Discus Palace, but there had been no mysterious fire, no hateful scrawl, no act of revenge. Simply fish, peaceful and blue in the deep and orange-cast night.

There was a midnight show of this loud, silly film—Newton wasn't allowed to stay later than that—and the crowd was going in, chatting on phones, buying candy and soda and hot dogs. Long lines. Newton, peaceful and smiling, didn't see Florence, she was too quiet, she could do that, and Newton was occupied with making change.

Florence sat on the stuffed bench next to the video games— Lee, Lee never even played video games like the other kids, always onto something else, money—where she could hear Newton's voice, see his profile.

He was so careful. He repeated each item as it was asked for—large coke, small popcorn, gummy bears—then punched the buttons on the register, and then, as he'd been instructed, read back the entire order. When all were agreed, Newton asked—had to ask—would you like to try the Coronet special? No one knew what this was, and they all refused. Too bad, they could've saved a lot if they'd asked. Finally, Newton assembled the order, tendered the cash, meticulously re-counted the change. Newton worked very hard.

The woman at the counter now had been snippy from the get-go. She had a snippy face, snippy hair cut, even her coat looked impatient. Said the words too fast, sought exasperation. When she repeated her order, she spit the words out like coins—large popcorn, small diet coke, good *and* plen-ty.

Did she want the Coronet special?

No, she did not, she wanted a small diet coke, large popcorn, and good and plenty, and she wanted it some time this year.

One thing about Newton's slowness, her tone of voice would not settle on him.

Yes, ma'am, he said.

While he assembled her order, the woman stared at Newton, her face growing snippier with every breath.

Newton began to count out the change—the thin bills evading his fingers—but it had all gone on too long, and the woman stole the money from his hands, saying, give me that, you moron, jeez, I swear, some people.

This Newton got, and he bent down behind the counter, pretending to look for supplies. When he stood up again, Florence knew he was confused because it was all out of order, Newton asking right off, would you like the Coronet special?

Florence rose, followed the woman, who stopped for napkins, and tapped her on the shoulder, Florence's other hand already rising, fast, out of nowhere. The slap was perfect, trebly, sharp and resonant, and before Florence could wait to see the woman's reaction, Florence was turned, gone out the door, and down the sidewalk and into the theater's parking lot.

Florence felt the slap for a long time, the sharp scratch of the woman's face, the sting. Even after she'd gone back for Newton, driven him home, and tucked him into bed, she could feel the slap, solid and perfect.

Newton slowly fell asleep, gurgling sentences just beyond her understanding. In the aquarium above his bed, the fish—purple and yellow and green—nibbled at the glass, kissed it. Her son's room flowed with the reflection of the calm blue currents, broken now and then by jagged streaks of white light.

Hilltop Café

I should have gone much earlier. Tina was already in her second year at Lone Mountain, and I had yet to visit her. Kelli and I had both planned to help Tina move into the dorms the year before, but there was a partners' event that weekend. Can't miss, Nick had told me, heavyweight. So Kelli and Tina went alone with my promises to be there soon. The sad thing was, I went to San Francisco several times after that, but always on partner business, and didn't make the time.

I kept meaning to change all that, but it got changed for me. I was visiting Nick in San Francisco, to clean up some discrepancies, when it all became clear to me. During that trip, business became pleasure, as it always did with Nick and the partners, and I found myself on the floor of Nick's new place, watching Nick and his new girl, who was the same age as Tina for all purposes, maybe a year older. I saw something of Tina in Nick's girl, a girl from the agency, Stephanie. I had fucked up everything. Fucked everything up. I had a terrible feeling it might already be too late.

I wanted to hop in the car and drive over to Lone Mountain and find Tina—she was only three miles away, tops—but I was just smart enough to know I was in no shape. So I flew home, got things in motion on the paperwork that would dissolve my interest in the partnership, talked everything over with Kelli, then got in the car and drove north. I figured the drive would do me good.

When I got to the city, late on a rainy Tuesday—it's February, the heart of the season—I checked into the E-Z Inn on Geary, less than a mile from the campus. We used to live in the city, back when we were just getting started, when Tina was a kid, and I remembered the place, nothing special, just a plain motel, carports under tiny rooms, big neon sign, crammed into a little strip of motels on a big windswept boulevard, and surrounded by Chinese restaurants, Japanese restaurants, futon stores, a record store, liquor stores. I remembered driving by the place, and thinking it would be the perfect place to disappear to, where no one would look for you, that place you'd go when your life got too hard or dangerous or shameful.

Coming to the city on business since then, I'd never have stayed here. We always stayed downtown in some plush but hip hotel, put it all on the tab. Nick had three requirements for a hotel. Thick robes, a wine list we could damage, and an astounding view of the bay. We must have tried them all. But for this trip, basic cable and an ice machine next to the lobby seemed right.

I hadn't told Tina I was coming, and I certainly didn't tell Nick. It was early in Tina's semester, and I was hoping she wasn't into mid-terms yet, thought I'd surprise her, keep it casual. I didn't know where Tina and I were headed, but I figured it would be a long journey, one that couldn't possibly be accomplished in a few days; I just wanted to get started.

Nick was supposed to be out of town, fishing in Alaska with a couple of new partners, Peter and Wayne, two men I despised. They were going to land, Nick said, trout as big as Dobermans, and get up to the usual trouble. I begged off going and arranged for the dissolution papers to arrive at the various offices of the various lawyers involved. Kelli promised to lie should Nick call. Nick and I could talk later. I was trying to keep things straight.

After I checked in, I got some ice and diet cokes and settled into the room, which faced the rainy boulevard. I tried Tina, but no answer, then checked my pager. Three from Nick, all the same, and in our code. When there was big fun afoot, Nick always punched in 69, he thought this was hilarious, and that meant I should call back and get on my way. The messages this night were 7734, which upside down spelled "hell." This was an emergency code red, top of the line, no excuses, life and death. But not tonight. I called Kelli, checked in, and she wished me good luck.

After several more tries, I got through to Tina.

"How's my kitten?"

"Daddy, what's the matter, is Mommy all right?"

"It's all good, it's just me, and I'm in town. Over here at the E-Z Inn. I thought we could spend a little time together. How about lunch tomorrow? Then dinner, too. You show me around. We can catch up."

"The E-Z Inn? Oh, Daddy, that's great. What a dive. Can we have lunch there, in your room. It'd be so cool. What're you doing here?"

"I miss you, and I'm taking a little break. Let's have lunch at the faculty club. I'll make reservations. One good for you?"

"Perfect. But what are you doing here, though?"

"To see you, Kitten, that's all. I swear. No business. I just thought..."

"Great. I'll be there, but I have to go, okay? Big night. I love you."

"I love you, too."

The rain was really coming down. I drank diet coke and stared at the pink and green neon mirrored in the asphalt, listened to the swish of the cars. Across from the E-Z Inn was a Korean barbecue whose name I couldn't make out. Above the store front were two floors of apartments, at least they looked like apartments, I could see TVs blinking in them, and I assumed the people who lived there were the owners of the restaurant. I stared at the front windows of those apartments for a very long time. From where I sat, it was clear that there were no windows on the deep side of the building. The two front windows on each floor were so small, maybe three feet by three feet, tiny tiny windows, and the only windows at all. I tried hard to imagine what life in such a place would be like. It baffled me that you could live in such a narrow world, with so little view. Kelli and I had made a nice house together, building and remodeling over the years, and we prided ourselves on the light, the windows we'd put in. We'd lived down south for years, in Eos, the valley of sun and heat, and had decided long ago to let it all in.

I was hungry all of a sudden, but too road-dead to go out. I found the number of the Korean place, called for delivery. A few minutes later, the guy stepped out of the front door, looked up and down the street, checked his tag, then looked across at the E-Z Inn, almost right at me. He bolted through the rain and cars, and when I answered the door, I could see he was amused by how short a trip he had made. I gave him a big tip, stayed in all night.

☙

Okay. The partnership. The agency.

Nick and I met in college, within a week we'd formed a partnership. It would take a while, we knew, to get it off the ground, but we were determined. We were going to loan big companies big sums of cash for short-term needs at outrageous rates. Big, quick scores, in and out, no commitments, all our money up front. After college, we set out to build some capital, buy a few businesses for collateral and cover, make contacts. We worked at it for three or four years, then through Nick met some older guys who were impressed with the package and helped us finance the first few deals. After that, we were golden, Nick's actual words. Golden, he'd say, untouchable. We could have everything, and we tried real hard to.

All the time we played like frat boys. Nick and I both got married, yes, started families, and got into all sorts of trouble. It all went together. At the time it seemed the big fun we were always insisting it had to be, but truth be told it made things pretty hard. Kelli and I went through a lot.

Anyway, when Tina was six or seven, the partnership acquired the agency. Technically a talent agency, but no matter how you call it, it was what it was, an escort service, outcall massage, hookers. Procurement. We called it the agency, simpler that way. The last piece in the package. Golfing, fishing, too much drinking, coke and other stupid drugs, and girls. The whole enchilada, Nick would say, and we can write it all off. He thought he was something; we all thought we were really something.

The worst thing, I said I was doing it all for Tina, and I thought I believed it. I was going out there, working the long hours, the weeks away from home, even the parties, because, it was implied, that's where we made the contacts, found the next big fish. And doing it all for Tina, so we'd have a nice house, a secure house, and a future, a good future, we'd be able to send her to the best schools, give her a leg up. But how do you do that? Spend so much time away from the ones you're doing it for. I've carried this picture of Tina in my wallet for years now, still carry it, and every once in a while I'd take it out and stare at it and talk to it, tell her that I was doing all this for her. And believing it all the while. It's one of those photo booth shots, one cut out of four, and she's about two. This was the last one in the strip, the one where she'd finally learned to smile for the camera, to open up, unafraid of the whirring and snapping of the machine.

I wasn't an idiot either, well, at least I wasn't immune to the facts of what I was doing. I knew that I was selling women to men—even though my hands were clean, obscured by paperwork and account numbers—and I knew that most of the women the agency sold were girls really, young women, in college a lot of them. I could draw the equation on a blackboard, but I always let the middle part of the equation, where x finally does equal y, remain fuzzy. And always told myself I was doing it for Tina.

For years I was horrible about it, joined Nick in all our stupid games, sleeping with the girls, thinking it was part of the package, the perks, a proper compensation, thinking that somehow I was doing these girls a favor. But I got tired of it, couldn't handle the outright lies any longer, couldn't stand the strain it put on me and Kelli. I took a lot of shit from Nick for abstaining from the girls. But I partied just the same, continued to go on the bashes and binges, and maintained my interest in the agency. It was just business.

Then there was the night at Nick's new place. Nick had done

what he said he would never do, he got involved with one girl, Stephanie. Before then it was all different girls, auditions, he'd say. I used to cringe when he said that. Just before Christmas Stephanie got pregnant, and Nick bought her a place in the city, lower Pacific Heights. He swore Raquel would never find out, doubted that she even cared any more, pretty sure she had something going, too. It was an unspoken arrangement. I had known Raquel from the beginning, when we were all newly married, and I was pretty sure she would object. Fiercely. Nick and Raquel had two daughters a few years younger than Tina.

I'd come up from Eos to go over the agency books with Nick, the rest of the partners were off on some golden goose egg chase, and we ended up at Stephanie's. They both wanted me to see it, to see the baby's room. They asked me to be godfather. Then we drank champagne and got high, and danced in the gorgeous apartment, a terrific view of downtown. Nick insisted we call in one of the girls for me, and Stephanie volunteered her friend Tish, but I wasn't up for that, hadn't been in ages. Nick grabbed me by the neck and called me a pussy, and I sat down on the floor. Incredibly, we were listening to Bob Marley, all singing along as if the words were true to us.

And there I was, on the floor, up against the couch, drinking champagne that could feed a family for a month, and watching Nick acting like a kid with Stephanie, as if this is how they wanted it, as if this were a good thing to do, as if it would all turn out okay. They would have this baby, and life would be sweet. Nick was slow dancing with her, but as they turned in the middle of the floor, I saw a look cross Stephanie. She was looking at the walls and the furniture, almost measuring up where everything would go, who would sit where, when it all fell away from her, and she was a kid again, Tina's age, like I said, and I think all she saw at that moment was a big empty apartment. She was scared.

Earlier that day, in the agency office, Nick had been talking about her, and it wasn't this Nick here, it was a Nick I had come to loathe. He called Stephanie a slut, called her stupid, said it definitely wasn't his baby, and he was going to split the minute the kid was born. She could keep the apartment, it was all paid for, he'd figured out a way to expense it.

I hated Nick then. I'm pretty sure I still do. But I hated myself more. I had done nothing for Tina. And I was scared. I did not want her to end up in this apartment, not with a man like Nick, not with a man who wanted to be Nick. It had all gone on too long. We were officially too old for this.

Nick actually gave me the word for how I felt about my connections to the agency. He'd said of a deal that day, "untenable," the requirements of the deal, he said, were untenable.

$\mathcal{C}$

Raining all day. I wandered around campus until lunch. The faculty club was nice. Club chairs with brass studs and real leather, teak tables, art deco fireplace. Tina was late, so I ordered a martini and settled in, watched the rain.

The minute I saw her, I knew we were in some sort of trouble. I couldn't believe she'd changed so much since Christmas, then I realized I really hadn't seen her at Christmas, we were always passing in the dark. I hadn't seen her, I figured, since last summer, just before Kelli and I slipped off to Barbuda. That

Tina, last summer's Tina, was still the same one I'd sent off to college, hanging around the pool all day, out with her high school buddies at night. She seemed to like college well enough, though she complained rather righteously about having to do work-study in the cafeteria for spending money, which we thought would be a good lesson for her. Last summer she dressed as she'd always dressed and seemed to be going in the right direction. We did get a letter from her last fall, a very long letter in emphatic pen detailing her decision to switch from Business to Cultural Studies, a choice neither Kelli nor I was thrilled with. Kelli wrote to Tina, expressing our concerns but giving our blessing. That change, though, could not have prepared me for the Tina who came blowing into the faculty club.

"Daddykins!"

She was giggling unaccountably. She had dark, dark circles under her eyes, her skin was washed of any tan. And her clothes. Thrift shop by the pound stuff. High top sneakers, a paisley tablecloth of a skirt over black leggings. Scarves and t-shirts and jackets, hard to figure out. Lots of cheap silver jewelry, bugs and skulls. But especially her hair, no, it wasn't blue, that I could deal with. It was cut in an awful bowl shape, boyish, amateur.

We hugged, and I couldn't tell if she'd gained or lost, couldn't find her in all those layers. I pulled away to look into her face, to smile at arm's length, but she spun away so fast.

"Isn't this ginchy?" she said. Ginchy was one of our old words together, from when she was a kid. Kelli used to roll her eyes a lot when Tina and I talked. She meant the Faculty Club, but I couldn't convert her tone into meaning. She was either being immensely sarcastic or perfectly genuine, and there was just no telling.

The whole picture confused me, except for one thing. Tina was high as a fucking kite. Though which drug was unclear. I knew this wasn't her first time, but I'd never seen it so extreme. We'd talk about this later.

"It's ginch-o-rama, Kitten. Ginch. O. Rama." This was another old thing we used to do. "Let's eat. I'm so glad to be here. Way past due. Nice school, by the way."

"You're paying for it."

I had the duck and she had the rabbit, wine for both of us.

"Mmmm, bunny," she said, somewhat maniacally, she was always a funny kid that way. She attacked that bunny.

She ate with her headphones on, but there was no music coming out of them, so I let it slide. We were talking about the usual things, mom, school, boys, music, and it all seemed to be going well. That was what I'd wanted. Just a normal day, a normal conversation, get settled. There would be time to go deeper.

We were alone in the club now, except for the wait staff. Tina stabbed a spear of asparagus and waved it in circles in front of her, staring at it as if the pattern she described held an answer for her. I could hear rain on the skylights.

"Dad, why are you here? Really?"

"I came to see you, Kit. Why so much trouble with that?"

Tina accused me with the asparagus.

"It's just been too long, is all. I've missed you."

I had to pause for a second, take a deep breath.

"You see," I said, and I wiped the corners of my mouth with my napkin. "I haven't been around enough lately, and well, things are changing with work, and I'm going to calm down a little. Spend more time with you."

The asparagus again. I wanted her to knock it off.

"So, no business at all? Not even Uncle Nick? Not even the agency?"

"No, that's all done with. I'm stepping away from the partnership. Nothing serious, just time for a change."

"You're giving up Uncle Nick?"

"In a way, yes."

"Good. You need to relax more."

"Why thank you. So, how about showing me around some, then we'll catch dinner tonight. Your choice."

"Oh, Daddy-o, I gotta go. Class. Chaucer. But tonight, for sure. I'll pick something really expensive. Ease your guilt and all, okay. Say seven. Hilltop Café. It's by the dorm. San Nicolas. Ask anyone. Bye. Yippee. I love you."

She kissed me on the cheek and was gone.

⁓

I asked the waitress if the patio was open, and I finished my wine out there under a beige umbrella and safe from the rain. The patio was enclosed by a high stucco wall that hid it from the rest of the campus. There were two lemon trees in terra cotta planters.

Sitting out there, in the now heavy rain, the clouds gray as gray can be, I had the glimpse of a memory I had been having for years. But only ever a glimpse, a hint. This memory was of a rainy day, some time ago, I know, but not that long, not from my childhood. For the briefest moment, and at the oddest times, this memory would creep into my brain, but before I could learn anything about it, it would disappear.

I'm on another patio, and it's late afternoon, the rain like string, and the patio is surrounded on three sides by wooden walls and sliding glass doors. We're three stories above the street. I know there are people in the house, and that the house is in San Francisco, and that's all I can ever remember. The image of the patio is so strong it's haunting. I want to know whose house this is, when it is, what I'm doing here. I search and search, then whoosh, it all fades away. Some quality of light and rain, walls and sky unhindered by trees, all spark the memory. I turn inward and disappear for a moment, but can never get it back.

It must have been the quiet rain of the patio, the solitude, but that day at the Faculty Club, when the images came to me, they stayed, worked in a little deeper, and I could finally name the memory. Tina was the missing link, it was obvious, because that day in San Francisco in my memory, Tina had also been with me.

This is before Eos, we still live in the city, and we're at Nick's place to celebrate a big deal. Tina has just turned nine, so it must be February. Raining and a gray-blue blanket over everything. Tina and I are on the patio together, the party going full blast inside, and I have stepped outside to check on her.

She is sitting all curled up in a white wire chair under a Cinzano umbrella, looking out at the rain and sky above the house across the street. It's beautiful, the air intoxicating and generous, clean, and I'm trying to explain this to Tina, that it's beautiful. She won't talk. I'm standing behind her. I try to break the ice again. I feel her shoulder tense under my hand. Her back is so tiny.

Then she says, without looking at me, "Dad, you are such an idiot."

She flies into the warm lighted rooms, and I should run after her but don't because I know she is right, I know exactly what she's talking about. On her birthday, a month before, I was supposed to be home at six for her party, a few friends coming over for cake and presents. But that day there was a partner's lunch at a wine bar we owned, a private affair, and things got a little out of hand, and by seven I was passed out in the backroom. I didn't get home that night at all.

In my memory I stand on the patio, feeling bad about what I've done, wanting to tell Tina I did not mean to hurt her, that there would be other birthdays. I want her to tell me how to make it up to her. I want her to see how beautiful the rain is.

I was relieved that the memory had finally come to me in its fullness. I sat on patio of the Faculty Club for the longest time, almost thought I'd cry, and tried to soak it all in. Funny thing, memory, all the emotions came along with it, a great swell inside me, and the regrets that followed.

After awhile, the waitress politely asked me to leave, said she had to get to class, too, so I set out in my parka to explore a bit.

e⌒

From the summit of Lone Mountain, one of the tallest hills in the city, I could see all of San Francisco, the bay and the ocean for miles, even under the tight lid of the rain. But the real trick of the place was in all the smaller hills and grades that grew out of the big hill. At every step there, the view changed. When you turned one corner of a pathway, you'd find yourself in a secluded grove of dwarf oak, which would lead to a narrow sidewalk between high classroom buildings, which would lead you to an almost aerial view of another quad far below. With each of these shifting views, there would be a different mood, a different sense of enclosure or freedom, a completely altered sense of the whole plan.

I walked to the very top of Lone Mountain, where the dorms sat, to work my way down again. Turning out from behind the Biz Management complex, I was suddenly on the edge of the hill again, and could see, far on the other side of the campus, seemingly a dream mile away, but still quite close, a little patch of grass surrounded by flowering plum and stone benches. There was a girl dancing in the rain on this isolated patch of grass, and it was Tina. By the time I'd flown across the campus and twisted and turned through the paths, and found what I thought must have been the patch of grass I'd seen from above, Tina was gone.

When I first caught sight of her dancing, I was charmed by her movements, by such a lovely surprise, and I couldn't have guessed how old this girl might be. Then I grew alarmed. Standing on the grass where Tina had been dancing, and looking back up the hill and across to where I'd been standing, I felt, in an instant, that I could almost see myself there, and that it had been ages since I'd stood there and looked down on my daughter. I checked through all the nearby buildings for her, but she was still gone.

e

When I got to the E-Z Inn, I found a ton of pages from Nick. Hell, he was in hell, the numbers said. But I didn't answer for a while. I tried Tina, thought about Kelli, but settled for an hour of rain-soaked boulevard, and the small windows of the apartments over the Korean place. Maybe I could talk Tina into Korean.

But no. I had to talk to Nick, get it over the real way. Nothing else until then.

"Hank. Where the fuck have you been? What the fuck is going on, what's with all these papers? What are you thinking?"

"I thought you were in Alaska. Look, I'm quitting, the papers are pretty clear. I'm not asking for too much, you know that. I've got more pressing matters. It's that simple."

"You are fucking crazy. The money, man, the money. Is everything all right at home? Think about this, man."

"Nick."

"Mr. Moore, man, what the fuck is this about? Be straight."

"It's Tina. It's real bad. And no, I can't talk about it."

"Are you sure?"

"Nick. Look. You're her godfather. Do the right thing, okay? Let's do it. I'll talk to you later, I swear. When I'm ready. You've got your own family."

"Okay."

"Yeah, okay. I gotta go."

℮

The Hilltop Café was on the bottom floor of San Nicolas, the dorm where Tina lived. The café was a big open space, where all the dorm kids ate, and you could get a latté and cookies and ice cream, and racks of candy, purple and green and blueberry. Studying and flirting. The outside wall was one long, long window that looked out on a grass courtyard with tables and umbrellas. I couldn't believe all the umbrellas on Lone Mountain; that's where my money went.

The courtyard was hemmed in by a low wall, beyond which was a steep drop onto a hillside of eucalyptus and scrub. And beyond, a view of the San Francisco skyline, the bay beyond it.

When I got there, I checked at the mail desk. Strangers weren't allowed upstairs alone. No answer in her room. I left her a message and went to the café. No Tina there, so I hunkered at a table with coffee, the school paper, rain. The soccer team, it appeared, showed promise. I sat near the front window, watched the kids and the city.

I finally saw her. She came into the far end of the courtyard from a gate I couldn't see, but stopped at one of the wooden tables and sat under the umbrella. It was clear she hadn't seen me, clear she wasn't looking for me. Or maybe it was the glare from indoors—it was full dark out—and she couldn't see in.

I reached to tap on the window, catch her eye, get her out of the rain, but I held back. Tina was laughing again, talking to herself, or talking to the surface of the table. She was plugged into her music, but she wasn't singing, she was talking, amusing herself, making herself laugh.

Tina pulled a black pen and a small white pad out of the rumple of her clothes and began to write, in a tiny hand, I could tell. She was talking and writing and laughing, and it seemed like she was trying to write as small as she possibly could, as if she were imprisoned in a castle and trying to sneak news of her dire fate to the outside world, to someone who could right her wrongs.

Tina brought the pad to her lips, kissed it gently, then walked over to the wall. She began to tear pages from the pad, then dropped them over the wall onto the dark hillside. I squeezed through the register lines, through squads of students, trying to keep an eye on her, but I lost her for a minute, and by the time I got to the courtyard doors, Tina was gone. I checked the halls that led to the dorms, but no Tina. I checked the courtyard again, empty, but went out there anyway. I found the gate in the back, but that led to a parking lot filled with gleaming cars and nothing else.

I hung over the edge of the outside wall, to see if there were any paths there, but no, nothing but scrub and a few chairs that had been tossed over. At the bottom of the wall, on the high side of the hill, about six feet down, I saw the papers that Tina had thrown over, but just the white squares, not the writing, it was too dark for that.

e

The girl at the mail desk told me that Tina still wasn't answering. She also told me that Tina often took walks at night alone, rain or no rain. She was known for that. There goes Tina, people would say.

I wandered all over campus, looking for Tina. No one else was out; the rain was torrential now, cold, deafening. I checked the library stacks, nothing there I need. In vain I checked the gym. I wandered the halls of deserted classrooms and found no clues. Every fifteen minutes or so, I'd call her and leave another message. No messages had been left for me at the E-Z Inn. For hours I did this, every once in a while swinging past the dorms and the café. She was out in it, I was sure, and I knew I had to find her, otherwise it would all get worse, and keep getting worse.

Around midnight, I was too tired and figured she'd have to be going back to her room soon. The food lines in the café were closed, but the seating area was still opened, so I bought a watery hot chocolate from a vending machine and waited.

The rain relented finally. I walked out into the courtyard and found some stars between the clouds, watched the downtown which seemed so far away in the sudden clarity. I peered over the edge of the wall and found Tina's scraps of writing again. There was an old tree stump at the bottom of the wall, and guessing the distance in the dark, I figured I could make it down there and back using the stump. I knew I was foolish to even think about making the leap, but I was stranded here, waiting for Tina, and foolish or not, it seemed the right thing to do. I swung my leg over the wall.

The concrete of the wall was scraping the insides of my arms and my fingers were burning while I hung there for a minute, but I eventually found the old stump with my toe, and let go. My foot slipped off the stump and I tumbled into the scrub and slid down the hill six or seven feet, coming to rest against a eucalyptus. My shin was bleeding, I was pretty sure of that, and something had whapped my face pretty hard. I was soaked. But I had to laugh. The sharp and sweet smell of the eucalyptus grove was a cloud.

It was hard going back up the hill, dead branches and slippery leaves giving way under me, but I made it to the base of the wall, and was able to locate Tina's scraps of paper. Even in the dark, I could tell that her sentences had blurred and bled in the rain, were illegible. I stuffed a handful of the pages in my pocket anyway.

The stump was just tall enough for me to grab a purchase on the top of the wall, but when I jumped up, crashing my knees into the concrete for a boost, my fingers slipped off, and I fell back down the hill again. One more time for good luck.

I made my way to the bottom of the hill, sliding mostly, nearly falling. I came to a path that led me around the base of Lone Mountain, and from there I made it back to the Hilltop Café. Tina was waiting for me there, all apologies. She was perfectly dry, dressed in a pink robe and pajamas, and I could tell she was straight. Her eyes were sharp, focused, a little hard to read, though, still resistant. She'd blown me off because she was angry, but was sorry. She'd thought I was getting off too easy, but when she saw me, realized I was serious. I explained everything that had happened, told her the whole truth, and we stayed in the café, all alone, for some time. We were getting somewhere.

When we left, she stopped by one of the vending machines and pointed at the bottom row.

"Dad, do you remember Chuckles?"

This was a candy from my childhood, one I had loved back then, and I used to bring Tina a package of Chuckles whenever I returned from a trip.

"Look," she said. "They have Chuckles. Do you want some?"

Tina fished just enough change out of her pocket to buy one package, and we took that back up to her dorm room. She promised to find me something warm.

I had forgotten that Tina had moved into a single room this year and was surprised at how small it was, with only one narrow window in the corner. But from this window, she said, you could see it all.

Clear Lake

Taipei had never been a destination, not even an idea. Before the accident, Wyatt Porter had only known the city as a branch office, a box often left unchecked on company memos. But after the accident, after he and Kim had mourned together for that long year in the house in Los Gatos, after their divorce, when neither of them could see any way or reason to continue, Taipei was suddenly before him, an urgent and temporary posting within the company, a manager of his rank and salary. He said yes, expecting to be there six months, tops, but found no reason to come home.

He'd not been in California in six years, eight since he'd been to Clear Lake. Eight years since Josephine had drowned. Josephine, JoJo, Jo, his only child. She was four when she drowned.

Wyatt and Kim arranged to rent out the lake house, to weekenders and the summer crowd, boaters and fishermen, and a management company took care of the details, saw to the house when it was empty, which was most of the year. The small income only paid for taxes and upkeep, but Wyatt and Kim had decided early on to maintain the property. Just in case, is what they said.

They bought the lake house the year Jo was born. Things were good, they both had nice jobs, owned a nice ranch-style home in Los Gatos with two big oaks on the property and right up against the Santa Cruz mountains, and here came Jo. Wyatt's father died that year, and to everyone's surprise, left each of his children a substantial windfall. Wyatt and Kim had discovered Clear Lake through friends the year before.

Clear Lake was a bit cheesy, at least on the north shore. The south shore had a bit more gleam to it, an Indian casino and a concert resort. The north shore's biggest town was Lakeport, a gold-rush era downtown long faded. There were cafés, a new and used bookstore, a local history museum, tepid restaurants. The rest of the north shore was dotted with smaller towns, and like Lakeport, each showcased a row of shoreline motels, most built during the sixties. There was a genuine Dairy Queen in Lucerne, something out of childhood. Wyatt and Kim found it all charming.

They bought the house outright, a commitment they were proud of. They knew that life would move them around California, town to town, but they would always have the lake house, and Jo would grow up there. It was a small house, clapboard siding, squat, but inside dark paneling gave the place a snug cabin feel. There was a dock and a boathouse, and so they bought a boat. It was a lake, after all. A sleek in-and-out, a twenty-footer with a hard-shell canopy and an open bow. Could hit fifty when pushed. Perfect for tubing and water-skiing. They both learned to drive the boat, loved its power, the sunburnt feel of a hot day on the lake. From the beginning Jo had loved the boat, too, squealed and wanted to go faster.

Late last spring he and Kim decided there was no more just in case, and they decided, through letters, to sell it. They'd split the proceeds, simple enough. They'd kept things simple all along. A buyer was finally found, and Wyatt was coming back to sign the papers and clear out the last of their personal belongings.

e⌒

He spent two nights at an airport hotel, trying to shake the jetlag. He slept in thick forgetful hours and spent the rest of the time watching television, mesmerized by the wash of English. He woke up Thursday, got in the car and drove north out of San Francisco.

He got to Hopland just before lunch, an hour shy of the lake, but the prospect of the mountain grades, the slow hairpin turns and steep drop-offs, made him weary. He stopped in the shade of an old oak on the perimeter of a winery and napped in the car, waking five hours later, groggy but determined to go on. By the time he dropped out of the last grade and came into Lakeport, the afternoon had taken hold of the day, softening the colors, lengthening the shadows, and drawing the far shore, with its hulking Mount Konocti, closer. The lake was tricky that way. Only from the middle did it look as big as it actually was.

Wyatt stopped in downtown Lakeport, thinking he'd get some supplies, but couldn't bring himself to go to Fast Eddie's. He stretched his legs, got in the car and kept moving, but when he came to the lake house, he moved on through to Lucerne.

At the Four Spots, he sat at the bar, which looked out onto the lake, and drank Bud and ate two cheeseburgers. October was late in the season, especially for a weekday, but the lake might still get busy over the weekend. For now, a few other regulars at the bar, locals, guys in plaid shirts and jeans and tractor hats. Loud music, straight-up rock.

Clear Lake had once been clear. It was the largest natural lake in California, other than Tahoe, which was half in Nevada and so didn't count, as the locals had it. But some time in the eighties, someone emptied a home aquarium into the lake, and the few strands of Hydrilla in the tank for decoration, unopposed by any predator, multiplied quickly. Within three years, the lake was clogged with the weed. The lake was green now, clouded. Within a quarter mile of the shore, you had to be careful or the Hydrilla would ruin your prop or intake. Even out in the middle of the lake, where it was eighty feet deep, Hydrilla grew along the bottom in great forests, obscuring everything.

Still, Clear Lake was beautiful, especially in the evenings. The mountains that flanked the lake, close and steep on the north shore, were all wild grass and scrub manzanita, too rocky, hot, and arid for anything else but beauty. Typical California, more of a desert than most people thought. From January on, the wild grasses were a tangy green, but quickly faded in early April. For the rest of the year, the terrain was dusky gold and brown. In the evenings, the barren hills were purple and orange. Austere, dramatic.

℃

Taipei was perfect because it was so strange. There was nothing in the city, and Wyatt adamantly stayed in the city, that reminded him of home, not the language, the signs, the weather, the food, not a single intonation of light. This was more of a relief than he could have prescribed for himself. At first he lived in the company suites in a corporate hotel near the airport, but even here he found enough of home to be painful to him, a certain newness to the building and its furnishings, a pandering to American tastes. When the posting became semi-permanent after a few months—he excelled at the position, nothing to do but work—he arranged for an apartment downtown near the harbor, where he settled.

The harbor district lay pinched between two steep mountains, mountains Wyatt thought of as typically Asian, from a fat-brushed drawing, precipitous and domed. The streets of this narrow valley were knotted with buildings in canyons of five and six stories. Above the ground floors of the open-front restaurants and grocers and electronics outlets, apartments rose in perfect anonymity above the always busy, truck-choked streets.

Wyatt moved into one of these apartments, much to the chagrin of his fellow employees, both American and Taiwanese. He could do better, they told him, find something in one of the garden districts, away from the chaos, something more suited, they intimated but never said, to his station. His secretary, Xing, a modest and well dressed woman, offered to help him, offered to find the proper place and make the arrangements. He ought to be more careful. The harbor was a dangerous place to be alone.

It was the balconies that swayed him. Each apartment had a balcony that faced the street and the balconies of those apartments across the way. In the States, these balconies would be called lanais, a slab of cement enclosed by cement walls, with a steel, waist-high railing on the open side, the living room of the apartment behind a sliding-glass door. The apartments reminded Wyatt of Indian villages he'd seen in the Southwest, hive-like dwellings, suitable for bats or mud-swallows, useful and anonymous, defensible. Wyatt loved to sit on his balcony in a cheap wrapped-wire chair and watch the streets and his neighbors. His apartment was on the third floor.

When he wasn't at work or watching television, Wyatt sat on his balcony. The balconies of his neighbors were filled with ornament and use. Banners hung from most, gold and crimson, the good fortune colors, but also in lime and carnation pink. The banners were covered with ideograms that were indecipherable. Some balconies had strips of Mylar hung from them to frighten pigeons. Each balcony invariably had a small charcoal barbecue, though these were rarely used. And because his neighbors were mostly families, there were lots of plastic kids' toys, in pastel tones, aqua and mint and peach. And potted plants and trees, all unfamiliar to Wyatt. There were shrines, too, on the balconies, lighted niches draped with fruit and bowls of incense, though Wyatt never took the time to find out exactly who his neighbors prayed to. Wyatt's balcony was the only one without decor.

If he leaned against the railing and looked down the long street, he could see the harbor and the big ships at anchor there and imagine what cargo they carried, out to the world and in from it. He had always planned on walking down to the harbor, thought he'd like to make something of a habit of it, his daily constitutional, a stroll among packed bales and cartons, commerce with the broad ocean beyond, but he never did go there, not once. What most compelled him about the view of the harbor from his balcony was its distance from his apartment, and how that distance could alter, expanding and contracting under the light of a given day. At times the harbor was a far, hazy dream, at others close enough to read the characters on the stevedores' helmets.

The canyon of the street's apartments changed every day, the light that flooded it and washed the walls of the buildings, slants of light impossible to predict in a near tropical country. In the evenings, the air that filled the canyon of his street could become drenched with a certain tone—say, lilac or tangerine, even once bright lemon with copper clouds scattered above—and living in the world was living in an aquarium illuminated by artificial means and inhabited by wholly unfamiliar creatures. In the evenings, the balcony families were more careless of closing their blinds, and having already turned on the night lamps, exposed more of their lives to him. Wyatt loved the evenings here, created little histories for each of the families. He always turned away if he was caught looking because he didn't want to seem a bad neighbor.

Wyatt knew what he was doing with his life. He was hiding. And by hiding, trying to forget Josephine, and Kim too, and that whole life. As if by being still. As if by distance alone. He suspected he should have been acting differently, knew that there were others who got on with their lives after the death of a child, who found the therapists and the groups and the friends who would pull them out of the dark tunnel life had backed them into. There was a certain way to approach such a loss, with vigor and aggression, and that by such an approach he might reclaim his life. But there was a quality to this American brand of grief that seemed to him too martial, as if it were a war whose only victory could be annihilation. Wyatt knew he was not this kind of person, knew for certain that complete oblivion was not something he could live with. He could not erase Jo.

He went to work each day and tumbled the numbers until they were polished smooth. He ate lunch with his fellow employees, occasionally went to a party, joined where he could.

He ate breakfast alone in his apartment, but took the rest of his meals at a sushi restaurant on his block, Hotei. He was drawn there, he suspected, by the Japanese couple who owned it. Jun and Miko were a childless couple only a few years older than Wyatt who had come to Taipei a decade before, lured, they said, by a business opportunity they'd been unable to resist, Japanese cuisine suddenly desirable in a flourishing Taiwan economy. Wyatt didn't believe their story and smelled something of scandal in their past, a minor scandal or an accident, a shamefulness, some wedge in their lives. Miko waited the three tables, and Jun worked the sushi bar. They worked seven long days a week. Penance, perhaps. They spoke enough English to be Wyatt's only companions outside of the office, and they treated him affectionately, as if he were a cousin. Wyatt sat at the last place along the sushi bar, near the wall and always reserved for him. Sake, sashimi, and whatever was freshest that day, miso soup. What they all appreciated about one another, it was obvious, was their exile.

He'd found a perfect hiding place. There was no need to learn the native language, no desire. Wyatt's only investigation of Taiwan culture was one television show he watched regularly, Super Sunday, a game show, or so he believed, that aired on Sunday nights for four hours. The show featured a quartet of hosts on a sound stage buzzing with lights and smoke, and backed by a fake grotto-like rock wall. The show's hosts wore outrageous clothes, pointy and shiny, something from ten minutes into the future. The studio audience was made up entirely of teenage girls dressed in school uniforms. The show's band was a group of young Taiwanese boys dressed as dissipated American rock stars from the seventies. While the show aired, the screen crawled with rolling scrolls of ideograms, one row across the bottom, another horizontal on the left margin, but Wyatt was not certain if these were translations or commentary.

Super Sunday contestants had to answer questions, most of which seemed to be about Asian pop stars, while the four hosts seemingly made fun of their answers. Near the end of the show—this was the segment that most dismayed Wyatt— someone apparently out of the contestant's past might, or might not, appear from behind a revolving door, shrouded in jets of smoke. Quite often there was no one behind the door, and instead there appeared, on a little pedestal, a telephone. The phone would ring, and the contestant would answer, conducting a one-way conversation that almost always ended in tears, real sobbing. Who was calling, Wyatt could never figure out. It was only at these times that the four hosts behaved sympathetically.

After years of watching Super Sunday, Wyatt was no closer to understanding the game. Nothing in the facial expressions or hand gestures, nor in any other context, provided illumination. The game grew more mysterious each week, and it was this that comforted Wyatt, the feeling that the mystery of the game would grow and grow, endlessly.

When the position in Taipei was offered to him as a permanent one, he accepted without hesitation. He had decided he was tired of being an American.

She was screaming, or laughing, or gasping for air. Calling to him? Just out of his reach, he thought, one hand away. Or maybe six feet below.

She was wearing her sky blue bathing suit, the one with the white traces of flowers on it. Her red sneakers. Her arms and legs were so thin. He could see the blue veins on the inside of her arms. The lake that was swallowing her was dark green, the shade of the most common and least expensive jade.

She was reaching up for him. She was looking right at him. Her eyes were the same color as the lake.

He could see her for thirty or forty feet as she sank, a pale blue stone dragged to the bottom.

They had gone out early that morning, when the lake was glassy, smooth. The year before Jo had spent the entire week in a neighbor's pool, but was too timid of the lake to do anything more than wade at the beach or ride in the boat. Even when wading she held his hand or Kim's. Just before the last trip, Jo had said at breakfast one morning that she wanted to swim in the lake that year. They'd see, both Kim and Wyatt had said, but she cajoled them until they promised. Promised. She would have to wear a life jacket. Okay.

Out in the middle of the lake, they stopped and drifted and enjoyed the morning. The water-skiers were a lazy crowd, hungover, late-risers, and so they had the lake all to themselves. The day was a scorcher, late August was beastly. They'd swim a little, eat lunch on the boat, spend the afternoon in the pool.

Wyatt got in first, the water was already warm. He paddled

around, showed Jo there was nothing to be afraid of. Kim guided her down the ladder, holding onto the shoulders of her life jacket, and Wyatt guided her feet from below until she was in the water. She clung to his neck for several minutes, afraid to let go but not panicking. That was the great thing about Jo, she knew when she was afraid of something, and her awareness of that fear gave her the courage to make it past the fear, to face it in her own good time and conquer it. She was a trooper.

Kim stayed on the boat, posting the orange caution flag and keeping an eye out for other boats. The lake under and around them seemed infinite, incapable of shore or bottom.

Gradually Jo relaxed, let herself float in the circle of Wyatt's arms, then drifted inches away, holding only his hands. They stayed close to the boat. Kim joined them.

"Daddy, can I ask you a question?"

"Of course, Jo."

"How deep is the lake?"

"Eighty feet probably. Out here."

"Is that a long way?"

"Very."

"Is it more than a googolplex?" A word she'd picked up in pre-school.

"Oh, yes," Wyatt said. "It's very deep, deeper than anything."

He was pushing her away from him, but still held her hands, drawing her near again, her feet landing on his knees.

"Why is it deep?"

"Well, some fish are very smart, and they like to hide there so they don't get caught."

"Are we fish?"

"No. We're ducks. We float."

"Hold me."

"Okay."

And he did, held her for a long time. He held her every time she asked.

"I'm ready to float now, Daddy."

"Okay, Jo. Float."

And he pushed her away, let go of her hands.

"See" he said. "You're floating, way out here in the middle of the lake."

She paddled to him, grabbed his hands, and said, "again."

He pushed her away, she paddled to him again, called "again again," and they kept doing this, her drifting off, paddling back, until Jo was six or seven feet off. Kim was paddling near the boat.

Then.

Then he turned to Kim—away from Jo—and said, "look who's a big girl, look who's swimming all by herself in the middle of the googolplex deep lake."

And then.

And then he turned back to Jo, but when he was turning, saw a look cross Kim's face at the same time he heard Jo cry out, and when he was done turning, Jo was not there, only the orange life jacket, turned on its side, and a little splash of the lake water.

Wyatt leaped out of the water half a foot, then knifed into the water, and he saw her, crying out, gasping, laughing, screaming, a string of bubbles rising, and she was looking at him, right at him, and reaching out for him. He could almost touch her. He kicked hard with his legs and pulled with his arms, but his feet were still out of the water. He righted himself, unbuckled his jacket—it took too long to unbuckle the jacket—saw Kim had done the same and was already gone. He dove back in. He watched Jo fall down and away from him. He shot back to the surface, gasped and dove, thought he saw Jo one last time, a blue flaw in the lake's jade, then lost her.

They continued to dive, but there was nothing. Kim tried to flag down help, while Wyatt swam and dove. Nothing.

The life jacket seemed fine, none of the under straps were torn or broken, and the buckles were all clasped. She must have wriggled free, maybe one of the straps had missed going around one of her legs and she'd dumped out the side. Kim and Wyatt both believed the jacket fit properly. If she had been screaming or crying, her lungs would have filled up and dragged her down, that and the weight of her red sneakers. They were assured that they had done nothing wrong. It was an accident.

Wyatt was pulled out of the lake by a couple of fishermen who'd come to Kim's flag waving. When they arrived, he was punching the water, hitting it with all his force, and yelling, and he was tiring, taking on water himself, and vomiting. Kim and Wyatt sat in their boat together, huddled under a large towel.

Fish and Game never found Jo's body. If she sank all the way to the bottom of the lake, she was probably tangled in the Hydrilla forest there, and she might never be found.

℮

The surface of the lake was perfectly still, without a single ripple. Just past dawn, not a single boat. Mount Konocti on the south shore was black, and so was the surface of the lake. The western hills behind the lake house were purple. Wyatt walked down the narrow dock to inspect the boat and the boat house, the hydraulic lift.

It had been dark when Wyatt arrived the night before. The crunch of the gravel on their driveway thrilled him, reminded him of other times when the crunch of gravel meant they'd arrived. A sensor light guided him in. That was new. The slight must of the cabin also told him that he was back, a cabin-y smell, a weekend smell.

After checking the pilots on the heaters—everything working—he checked the bedrooms, fresh sheets, then went back to the kitchen. The lights there were too bright in the dark of this night. He opened a drawer, a silverware drawer, a ragged collection of utensils. Nothing fit, but everything was useful. That seemed enough, so he went to bed, slept straight through until just before dawn. He was adjusting to the time gap. As he always had when at the lake, when he got out of bed, he went down to the shore.

The boat house, elevated above the lake's surface, was in fine shape, and the boat, too, everything clean and fit, no clutter. The windows of the boat house were startlingly clear. Wyatt punched the fuses and tested the lift, which purred. He unsnapped the boat from its moorings, lowered it halfway, raised it again, re-secured the works. He knew the boat would fire up right away.

Walking back up to the house, Wyatt found that very little had changed. There were no new houses on the cove, and he had fully expected there would be, but still the same twelve houses, each with a dock, each house tucked into a grove of pepper, willow, and California oak to guard against the intense summer heat. A few of the houses looked newly painted, there were a few more jet-skis on the gravel beaches, and the grove of Eucalyptus across the road, up against the steep hillside, seemed larger.

Their house looked terrific. Whoever was tending to it was doing a great job. Wyatt knew it had been re-painted, but the tiniest details had also been looked after. The screens in the windows were fresh and true. The paths in and around the garden were filled with new gravel that was raked and tamped, and the garden itself was in better shape than Wyatt had ever seen it. There were no weeds at all, the juniper hedge was trimmed. Just beyond the garden, the trash cans were lined up neatly by the carport. Every window of the house was immaculate, affording him a view of the interior, which was orderly and cozy. It amazed Wyatt that the house could be in such fine shape, that something he possessed, but had neglected for so long, could remain pristine. Untouched, as if time had not only been halted, as if it had been forced to run backwards for a while.

Out on the lake the first boat of the morning described a wide arc, the motor high-pitched, running hard, ripples re-ordering the surface.

e~

He turned on the kitchen radio, a new one, and found it tuned to the same old station, KLKE, a public broadcasting outlet in Lakeport that played jazz, bluegrass, and reggae. This morning it was jazz, a Les Paul album, small hammers on crystalline strings.

The refrigerator was stocked with food for breakfast and lunch, and the coffee maker was ready to go, the beans ground and the water poured. After bagels and blackberry jam and coffee and staring at the lake—it had been so long since he'd had either, a breakfast this big and fresh, and such a wide open vista—it was time to start what he'd come here to do. He would pack up all the things he and Kim had left behind. Tomorrow he would sign the papers and say good-bye to the lake.

But there was nothing to pack. He went from the living room into the two bedrooms, the bathroom, and back through the kitchen. There were books in the shelves and nightstands, but they were not Kim and Wyatt's, mostly thrillers and fantasies. The books in Jo's room were not hers either, they were for older kids, chapter books. This was a relief. He had dreaded picking up the books he used to read to Jo at night. He was afraid he'd find *Mr. Rabbit and the Lovely Present,* afraid he'd have to look at the picture of the girl and the rabbit sitting by the lake at dusk, all greens and blues.

The bed linens were different, and the towels and the shower curtain. The curtains throughout the house were changed, if not new, at least different. On his second trip through the house, he checked the closets, and in Jo's room found five cardboard boxes piled in a corner there, they'd obviously been there awhile, each box with the words "Porters—Do Not Open" on the side in black marker. His work was already done.

In the kitchen he found the only things of theirs that remained unpacked, the ragtag collection of spoons, knives, and forks, and a stack of cheap, plastic plates. The plates were mostly from fast-food restaurants and decorated with cartoon characters. The one on top of the stack had been Jo's favorite. It showed Hercules posing with one bicep flexed, an all-American gleam in his eye.

Around the edge of the plate was the legend, "the strongest guy in the world." He and Jo loved to say that together, in their sheriff voices, "I'm the strongest guy in the world."

Wyatt sat at the kitchen table, his head buried in his arms, and he wept.

℮

Just past noon, the day was already baking, at least ninety and getting hotter, unusual for October, but not uncommon. There was always one last hurrah of heat before the first rains of November arrived. Wyatt was sitting in the boat in the boat house, hovering above the lake, trying to decide whether to go for one last ride, when he saw a man coming up the dock. He was trailed by a teenage girl, obviously the man's daughter.

"Howdy, neighbor," the man called, waving. "You must be Wyatt. I'm from next door. I'm your caretaker."

Wyatt stood in the boat—never stand in the boat when it's hung up—and waved back. He sat down.

"Howdy," he said.

The man seemed much younger than Wyatt, but probably wasn't. He wore cut-off jeans, sandals, a yellow t-shirt with a dancing frog. His hair, a full brush of it, had been high-lighted by the sun; his arms and legs were tanned. Nut brown, that's what people said.

"Bob," he said. "Bob Preston, nice to finally meet you. Hope you found your breakfast."

Bob had taken over as caretaker for the management company a year or so back. He looked after five of the houses on the cove and another handful along the north shore. He and his family got to live in the house next to Wyatt's as part of their salary. It was a great deal, and they enjoyed meeting the renters and having time alone, too. He thought of himself more like an innkeeper than a custodian, he told Wyatt. Made it more pleasant for everyone that way. He'd keep looking after Wyatt's place even when it was sold. Good hands.

Wyatt told Bob he was doing a great job, the house looked really great. He appreciated the food.

"This is Rachel," Bob said. "Rachel, c'mon in, say hi to Wyatt, he's the owner here. Our daughter."

Daughter. The word rose up in Wyatt's throat.

The girl had been standing outside the boat house in the sun, and when she stepped inside, Wyatt could only see her silhouette. Then she appeared. She was tall for her age—if you saw her from the back, you could easily mistake her for a college student—but when her face became visible, there was no mistaking she was thirteen or fourteen. Cute, with braces and no attempt to hide them, a broad smile. Her hair was done up in a complicated set of French braids, and it looked wet from a swim, but Wyatt guessed this was just the gel she used. She wore a plain, oversized t-shirt, khaki shorts, no shoes, a toe ring.

She shook Wyatt's hand—delicate fingers—then shuffled a little closer to her father.

"Is this your boat?" she asked Wyatt.

"Now, don't start," Bob said, punching her in the arm. "She is just crazy about boats. A little embarrassed by ours. Not fast enough."

Rachel smiled again, turned away.

"Anyway, listen," Bob said. "We're having a little barbecue tonight, some of the cove folks, and wondered if you'd like to come by. Say four or five."

"That'd be great. Love to. I'm afraid to say it's been too long since I've been here. Don't really know anyone anymore. Can I bring something?"

"Just your old self. That'll do. Come on by."

"Hey, listen. I'm just gonna put the boat in, take her out for a spin. Wanna come?"

"I got to go to town and pick up a few things for tonight. Some other time."

"Let's take the boat. There and back. That way I can pitch in, help out. Yeah?"

"Sounds great. Rachel?"

She was already nodding.

Wyatt helped them in, gave them vests, got everyone seated, and lowered the boat onto the surface of the lake. It did start right up.

*

The house where Bob lived with his wife Celia and their daughter was smaller than Wyatt's, one bedroom, Bob and Celia's. Rachel slept on a fold-out sofa in the living room, which itself was just an extension of the kitchen. The bathroom had one of those plastic shower stall pre-fabs, the kind where the water gets all over the floor no matter how hard you try. Their beach front was a postage stamp, a tree-enclosed square of dirt and rock with a wooden picnic table that must have been original to the place, and a crumbling brick barbecue, also original. There was no boat house here, only a floating dock, at the end of which was tethered their boat, an aluminum twelve-foot with an outboard. Theirs was a troller's boat, nothing of the speed and power of Wyatt's.

Wyatt had never been to this house, never knew who'd lived here. The fat junipers had kept the house and beach hidden from their property. He and Kim had always imagined that, after years of coming up to the lake for weekends, maybe even entire summers, that they'd have lake friends and that Jo would grow up with the neighbors' kids. They were just starting to make friends. The Taylors, on the same cove, had let Jo swim in their pool. The Taylors, Bob told him, had moved away a few years before, back East.

Wyatt was the last to arrive at the picnic. He'd popped into Lucerne to pick up some wine. There were two other families there, both up from the city for the weekend and staying in other cove homes Bob looked after. They all shook hands and exchanged names but Wyatt promptly forgot them. They seemed like nice people, but they were occupied, quite gleefully, with their kids, a brother and sister set, maybe one and three, and a little tow-headed boy about four. The parents and the kids were splashing in the lake. Bob and Celia were tending the barbecue, burgers and chicken and corn. Celia was tall and thin, certainly Rachel's mom, except with blue eyes. Every once in a while Celia would lean against Bob, half affection and half fatigue, and every once in a while, Bob would raise his bottle of beer in Wyatt's direction.

The promise of the day had come to fruition, it was hot beyond baking. Scalding. Wyatt sat at the corner of the picnic table still enveloped in the shade. Rachel sat across from him, telling him everything he needed to know. They were both drinking supermarket brand diet sodas. Bob, according to Rachel, had been at loose ends for many years. They'd always lived here, Rachel was born here, but Bob could never find a job that suited him. He'd done construction, sold and rented boats at Wisney's World of Water, clerked in various markets, did seasonal work in the pear orchards and vineyards, and once had studied for his real estate license. A few years back, Celia had taken some temp work in a medical office, found she liked it, and was soon running the place. Bob stayed home for a bit, to figure things out, and took to doing spot chores at different properties. Bob found he liked being home, it fit him, and he was a much better dad, in Rachel's opinion, for staying home. He was an excellent putterer. When Bob hooked up with the management company and they moved to the cove, everything fell into place. Even Rachel's grades improved. Before they had lived in town, but the lake, well, just take a look for yourself. Who wouldn't love it?

Rachel's eyes were a brown that was hard to predict, hard to qualify. Chocolate was the word that first sprang to mind, but that was dead wrong, there was too much copper in them, undertones of orange and red flashing, especially when she was being funny. Finally, Wyatt decided that this was simply Rachel's color, one that she alone possessed.

She was an engaged kid, and this surprised Wyatt, he hadn't expected it of a fourteen year-old—she'd turned fourteen the month before. Instead he had expected her to be sullen, listless, too cool for anyone or anything. When Wyatt arrived at their place, Rachel was playing with the kids down by the lake, one minute goofy with them, the next minute stern and watchful. She talked to all the adults, even her parents. She peppered Wyatt with questions, and while he knew she was also buttering him up for another boat ride—he'd already determined to offer it—she was honestly curious, to no end. She was a good kid.

After dinner, Wyatt watched Rachel play with the little kids, and was amazed to find his heart wasn't breaking. He thought it should be breaking because Rachel was so close in age to what Jo would be now, Rachel some future ghost sent to haunt him. But she wasn't Jo's age, she was almost two years older than Jo would be. Rachel could have been her big sister, or a cousin, a cove neighbor, someone to look up to.

The adults were sitting at the picnic table, now in full late-day shade, and they were talking about the food, the heat, Wyatt selling the house. The others were delicate when talking about selling the house. It was obvious that they knew about Jo, that she had drowned.

Rachel was on the tiny beach all by herself now, staring at the broad, flat lake, wishing herself to the middle of it. The other kids were making a pile of rocks. It was only six, plenty of light left. Time for one last trip in the boat.

He said it aloud, to no one and everyone, but keeping an eye on Rachel.

"Who wants to go out on the lake? I'm driving."

Rachel couldn't have turned around faster. The other couples thanked him, but they were going back to their houses soon, bath time and book time and bed time. Bob and Celia were pooped, they said, a few chores still to do, but Rachel was welcome to go with Wyatt if she liked.

"You know," Bob said. "You have a tube, you could go tubing.

I keep it inflated for the renters. Things like that ought to be used. I replaced the tow rope last year. Safe as houses."

"Would Rachel like that? I can do that."

Bob was smiling the whole time. Excited, Wyatt imagined, that his daughter was stepping out a bit, getting to do what she loved.

"She would. And Wyatt, don't worry about her. She knows to be safe, and she is. She's a lifeguard. Did you know that?"

$\sim$

Out in the middle of the lake was a completely new day. Under the steep hills in the cove, everything was purple and orange, evening, but in the middle of the lake, with no mountain shadows, it was all clear light, and still close to ninety, no wind. Only a few other boaters were out, far away by the narrows.

Wyatt posted the caution flag. Rachel stripped down to her suit, a safety-red one-piece, and into her jacket, then slathered herself with sunscreen. She checked and re-checked the tow line, then lowered the tube into the lake. Wyatt held it close to the boat. She climbed down the dive ladder, then pushed off from the boat a ways.

"God, this feels great," she said. "Thank you so much. And you know I'll be careful, right? I promise."

Rachel bellied onto the tube, her legs hanging off the back of it, got a good grip, and Wyatt pushed her away from the back of the boat until the line was played out. Wyatt put the engine in gear, the rope went taut, and they were off. Soon he was cruising, cutting wide swaths in the lake, but never going fast enough to send Rachel outside the boat's steep wake. Rachel waved and smiled, and just kept going. After almost an hour, she signaled Wyatt with a cutting motion across her neck. She was ready to come back in.

After they stowed the tube and rope, Rachel asked if there were time for one last swim. She was a great swimmer, she wanted him to know, she was certified.

She took off her jacket and pushed into the lake from the top of the dive ladder. She swam in circles, diving deep and surfacing, whooping. Wyatt could see her the entire time, that red suit of hers. When she was done, she cajoled Wyatt to swim—one of them had to stay with the boat at all times—and he finally relented.

The water was cold at first, and Wyatt kept his head dry, but soon little patches of warm current crossed his body, invisible currents in an otherwise still lake. Warm, cold, warm, cold, the temperature was always changing. Just before he got out of the lake, Wyatt took one dive, fairly deep, and he was okay. There was nothing in the lake except water.

℮

By the time they got back in the boat, the evening was over everything, the sun just behind the barren mountains. Wyatt let Rachel drive until the quarter-mile buoys. She was remarkably good. She asked him, while she drove, a ton of questions about Taiwan. He had very few answers for her. "That's okay," she said. "You can tell me later. When you get back, take some notes and send me a letter. Okay?"

He dropped her off at her parents' beach, where they were sitting at the picnic bench. He was trying to inch the big boat close to the dock, but Rachel had a better idea.

"Okay," she said. "Absolutely my last swim tonight." She tossed her clothes on the dock, and Wyatt pulled away from it, farther from the beach.

"Thanks," she said. "That was great."

"Maybe we'll go out in the morning," he said. "I don't have to be anywhere till noon."

"Cool," she said. "And listen, you should come back. I know you sold the house and all, but you should still come here. I told you the lake was beautiful."

Wyatt cut the motor, and Rachel jumped off the dive ladder, dove down into the lake, and swam quite a ways under the water, surfacing close to the beach. She stepped up out of the lake, dripping, obviously cold, but her mother was waiting for her with a towel. Wyatt called out that he would see them in the morning. The house was all lit up behind them.

He turned on the running lights and headed to the quarter-mile buoys. Once he crossed the buoys, he throttled up and headed out into the lake again.

Soon it would be night, moonless, and he wanted to be out there. The stars were unbelievable at night in the middle of the lake.

He pushed the boat, it sped up, and in only a moment he hit that speed where the bow lifts up out of the water and you're almost flying. The boat rises, you take off. Out across the black lake.

When he got back to Taiwan, he would travel. One of Rachel's questions had been, what was the most beautiful place in Taiwan?

Xing was always telling him about Sun and Moon Lake, deep in the country's south. It was a big lake, she told him, but what made it special were the islands, hundreds of them. Most of the islands were so small there was barely room for a shrine, but that's what people put there. Each island was a sacred shrine, and at night, all the shrines were lit up. It was a beautiful trip, she told him, to hire a small boat and cruise from island to island.

Wyatt would go there first, and he'd send a postcard to Rachel. He'd ask questions, too, and read books and take notes. And when he returned to Taipei, he'd write her a long letter.

He would do his best to find out about this lake. He would find out what the shrines were for, how people honored them, what gods they were dedicated to.

An American Son

I.

You might remember me, but I'd doubt it. Once, long ago, I captured your attention for several weeks, but soon after you forgot me, and with a great persistence. You're good at that, America. Forgetting.

My name is Robert Macoby. No? I'll tell you then, and more.

In February 1974, when I was seventeen, a high school junior in an average cold war working-class suburb of San Jose, California, I defected to the Soviet Union. Good word that, defected. I had already decided, at fifteen, having discovered Steinbeck, that I would devote my life to writing, that I would indeed become a great writer, and for a couple of years worked on stories and a novel in perfect adolescent innocence, until one day my stepfather spelled out the long odds against my literary success. America, he told me plainly, was no place for writers.

I had read Solzhenitsyn, of course, and others, and as a Sputnik baby, 1957, grew up surrounded by images and imaginings of the godless Soviets; it was difficult in the middle of the last century not to be compelled, in some fashion, to the black and white world of that dystopia. I knew that in Russia literature, at least, mattered. A few years before my defection, eight hundred Muscovites waited all night outside a bookshop for a recently liberated edition of *Anna Karenina*, and by the end of that day, in a country where no one could afford it, every known copy of the book was sold.

On a rainy February evening, I stole out of my stepfather's condo, rode my bike to the train station in downtown San Jose, took the train to San Francisco, spent my last five dollars on a taxi, and presented myself at the Soviet Embassy on Green St. where I pled my case for political refuge. By three that morning, after a rather perfunctory interview with a top consular official, I was on a fishing trawler headed for a Soviet submarine, and from there to Moscow, where I have lived the past twenty-six years.

I was all the rage for a while. Microphones and cameras swooped down on my mother and stepfather, yearbook photos of my smiling self appeared in newspapers around the world, news conferences and talks shows convened—what had gone wrong? Lights burned in embassies, consulates, safe houses, bodies politic as distant as Yemen. But no stand-off, no accusations; it was clear I was not unwilling or uncared for in the matter. I appeared on Soviet television and in Soviet periodicals where I happily embraced the people's revolution. My mother continued to make public pleas for my return, although in our private phone calls, I assured her I was fine and happy. I was happy; Moscow was everything I hoped for.

American amnesia is a peculiar variety, not merely the act of forgetting, attrition, but an amnesia of surplus, bounty, the next big story drowning out the last with its own urgency and colorful cast of characters, innumerable details, spins. In 1974 you had nearly forgotten Vietnam, a war not even over then; certainly my small adventure would also fade.

In June of the same year, surrounded by well-wishers after a performance at Toronto's O'Keefe Center, Mikhail Barishnikov slipped away from his handlers and into a waiting car that sped him into the dark Canadian forest and a private country estate. How could I compete with Barishnikov, his exile, his defection so much more picturesque than my own? Then in August, Nixon defected to his own Siberia on the foggy beaches of San Clemente, and the trump was complete. Would I have been forgotten if Barishnikov weren't so beautiful, Nixon not so grotesque?

None of this matters any longer, it barely mattered then. Today, Barishnikov is the consummate American, dead Nixon the revivified saint, and I've had a fruitful career in Moscow, my books abundant, albeit in Russian. Thriving in exile, each of us.

I have lived in the same modest Moscow apartment since my arrival, and each morning since, I have sat at this same scarred table in Café Zhelanye, with a cup of gritty Kava, looked out the same cracked and iced windows, and written tales of my America, longhand in the same Soviet-green notebooks. I have written with the same pen, too, a gift from the Writers Congress upon my arrival, a pen that is sturdy, indestructible really, MiG green. The pen and the notebooks are each stamped with the martial Red Star of the East. After the Soviet Union collapsed—evaporated— Russians continued to read my books, I've been fortunate in that. It's been as good a life as I could have expected. But tomorrow will be different. I'm coming back home, a citizen of the world, holding my own passport, traveling alone and unknown. You have something of mine, and I mean to retrieve it.

Don't underestimate children, how much they know of the world. At seventeen I knew more than most about the Soviet Union, and was never naive to its terror and depredations. But I had my reasons for going, good reasons.

My father died when I was thirteen. Elwell Macoby, Mac to his pals, career Navy man, CPO, Master Diver, had retired when I was seven and moved us back to San Jose from our last post in Key West. For the next six years he moved from job to job, employed as a welder, slowly discovering that the San Jose he'd returned to had no real use for men of his generation. He was employed, yes, but granted no future; the future belonged to men like Bob, my soon to be stepfather, a man enamored of electronics and plastics, a man who'd missed the war by a couple of years.

The last two years of my father's life, he was spottily employed, one part-time job or another, eventually reduced to sharpening knives on weekends in the hardware department of Sears Roebuck, a man who'd built ships, who'd touched the bottom of the ocean. My mother and I did not know that my father was unemployed. He continued to pay the mortgage, put food on the table, clothes on our backs, what was needed. My father often took me out of school those last years, without my mother's knowing, and we'd go off fishing or hiking up near Mt. Uhmunuhm. I'm certain it was these years that killed him, the weightlessness of unnecessary tasks. If a diver rises too quickly through the stages of oceanic pressure, his blood will fill with nitrogen and kill him. Mac Macoby had lied about his age to join the Navy at fifteen, to save the world from evil, and to rise above his own sharecropper past. He found a home there, in the military order, and under the sea. The ascent to civilian life had been too rapid, too without the pressure he was used to. On May 5, 1970, his blood thickened and stopped his heart.

We buried Mac in the veteran's plot of Oak Hill Cemetery, across the way from the General Electric plant where he once fabricated nuclear reactor shells. My mother and I lived suddenly alone, getting used to each other and missing him. It's not that we disliked each other, but in the last years of my father's life he and I had grown close, and I'd necessarily drawn away from her. What we had in common was my father's absence, and that was enough for a while, until we ran out of ways to say that we missed him, and I began to see in her eyes, over the early dinners we shared in silence, that the order of her life had also been kicked from under her. Her smile, wan at best then, was a simple question, what shall I do without your father. I'd been a late child in their marriage, and my mother was in her forties when Mac died. What would she do? I began to dread our time together. Christmases were the worst.

Two years later my mom met Bob at church, he was a widower of six months, and a year after that, they married and we all moved into the brand spanking new condo complex, Rendezvous West.

Bob the Blob. Or simply Blob. He wasn't fat, really, though a tad corpulent, stuffed into his blue suit as if he'd been born in it. Blob because he wasn't my father and could never hope to be, poor man, and because our names were too close, I'd have none of that. Yes, I called him Blob to his face. With a smile.

Blob was the opposite of my father, staid and secure, home every night, gifted with the knack of having a job deemed necessary, and my mother grew into Blob quickly. Within the first few months of their life together, they took to wearing identical powder-blue track suits and were soon indistinguishable.

Blob worked in the Blue Box, a large blue-glassed cube of a building near Moffett Naval Air Station, whose purpose and products were never quite clear to outsiders. Blob would only say, "Can't tell, national security." I asked him maybe a hundred times, honestly curious, "Blob, what *do* you do?" He never did tell, a surprised pride in his silence, as if the security of the free world might actually rest with him.

We settled into our new lives, ensconced in the oak grove foothills of the Santa Cruz mountains. Rendezvous West—pool, spa, tennis, reasonable adult living. For my mom's sake, I got along with Blob, a not too difficult task; after all, the man had no edges. He wasn't awful, he was vague. My mother was relieved by Blob, thrilled to be exempt from the rogue life of the Navy and the sullen rage and folly of my father's that followed it. I did not feel betrayed by my mother, it was clear enough Blob was what she needed, and I was more than happy to cling to my father's memory alone.

Blob bestowed much upon me and furnished our lives in a manner that could only be described as lavish. For starters, he presented me with the condo's master bedroom, and yes, this gesture does, and did then too, seem slightly oedipal. The master bedroom was not only enormous, but it offered escape, as if Blob were tempting me to run away. "Look," Blob said, "it even has its own sliding door, and we trust you with it." The view from the sliding door was superb, past a short fence, a long flat path through a shallow valley of oak and grass. The grass was gold straw in summer, nearly white by August, and in February a green so intense it made my teeth ache. On full moon nights, owls swept fruitfully up this path.

Blob was the stepfather you couldn't even dream about. He never asked questions and he lavished me with gifts. The most imposing of these gifts was a stereo as colorful, complex, and loud as the cockpit of a jet. To spite him, I rarely used it, and preferred my old AM clock radio, yes, the one my father had given me.

I went to school every day, a new school in a different district, stayed in touch with a few old friends, walked up and down the live oak valley, dreaming of Steinbeck's lost valley, and at night, shut myself in my room and wrote stories about lonely teenagers and dead fathers, while listening to the mysteries that only AM radio can provide, stations from Los Angeles, Mexico, Chicago, occasionally China or Japan, and once, Russia. Self-stuck in a one-room world, dreaming of far-off places to cracked radio tunes. Ready to defect.

℮

The decision to defect came sharply one day and was executed that same evening. Mom, Blob, and I were out for our regular Saturday shopping day at Valley Fair, the biggest, newest mall in the Santa Clara Valley. Mom was doing the actual shopping, while Blob and I were set adrift on a sea of polished stone floor with the other men. My only stop on these shopping days was the B.Dalton Bookseller, where I knew Blob would spring for anything.

A year before in this same bookstore, Blob had bought me Solzhenitsyn's *Gulag Archipelago* in hardcover. In one year I had zoomed through all of Steinbeck and London, had read all of Hemingway's war romances, and I was casting about for a new feast. Blob put the Solzhenitsyn in my hand, a silver brick of a book. He had read something of it in the papers and figured it must be good, and well, didn't I like books, but I wasn't hearing his sales pitch, I was already in love with it, the slick dust jacket, the paper smell, the endless river of pages. I did nothing for a week but read *The Gulag*, cut school a few days for it, and immediately searched for other Soviets, Pasternak, Bulgakov, Mandelstam, Akhmatova.

Not as strange as you might imagine. I already had a predisposition for the dystopic. When I was eleven, my sixth grade teacher read to us, on long sleepy spring afternoons, from *A Wrinkle in Time*, about time-traveling kids transported to worlds of stultifying sameness and terror; a year or so later, the late night movies gave me Truffaut's "Fahrenheit 451," followed by Bradbury's book of the same in high school; *Animal Farm* and *1984*, to be sure; and Huxley's *Brave New World*, a book custom-made for a kid like me. These books gave me a yen for worlds in which it was possible to live heroically.

At Valley Fair, on my last day in the U.S., Blob did it for me again. "Look," he said, "here's part two of that book you like so much, let me buy it for you." He wanted to buy me the hardcover of *Gulag II*, but the book was also published as a small paperback, and that's the edition I wanted, the print as cramped as possible. Solzhenitsyn, during his time in the camps, wrote on the tiniest scraps of paper, and I wanted to pretend that I was a prisoner, that my covert reading was a necessity of survival, but Blob would have none of it. We could afford the hardcover, and he didn't want me to hurt my eyes.

Then Blob wondered if we might sit down together, have a little talk. This was scary for being surprising, we'd never had a little talk before, and I knew he meant by little talk a big talk. We sat near the waterfall in the dead center of the mall, on stone benches with green and orange gurgling streams at our backs. Shoppers swarmed our view.

"Robert, your mother and I have been talking about your future, and we thought it was time we share our views with you."

"Yes, sir," I said brightly. I was nothing if not polite.

"Now, I know..." he said, and he put his hand on my shoulder, awkwardly, as you'd suspect. "And your mother knows, too, that you've got your heart set on going to college, and on this whole writing thing. But, let me be blunt. I will pay for your college, as we've already discussed...*if* you decide to go into engineering or business. Your mother and I think it just doesn't make sense to pay for college so you can chase this particular dream. Writing never put food on the table or paid the mortgage.

He waited me for to object, but how could I? He was right.

"I know this is a bit of a surprise, but there's good news, too, and I think you're going to be thrilled. A good friend of mine, he works over at Lockheed, and he's a *professional* writer, technical writing, you see, computers, weapons systems, all that. I've told him about you, and he's promised to take you on the minute you graduate college. You'll be a writer *and* making good money. He'll show you the ropes."

Poor Bob. He looked so tired just then. I almost felt I should argue with him, he'd put so much effort—good hearted effort—into our little talk. But he was tired; I wanted to let him rest.

"That's a very interesting offer," I said. "And I appreciate it.

I'll consider it very carefully. Thank you very much."

"Well, then," he said. He seemed puzzled. "Good," he said. "Good, that's great. Fine. Okay."

I made up my mind right there, a simple choice for me. By the time we got back to the condo, I'd mapped it out. Bike, train, taxi, submarine, Russia.

Looking back from here, in Café Zhelanye, I can pick apart the threads of the reasons I defected. I've told you some of them. But on that day, riding in the backseat of Blob's Montego, heavy Solzhenitsyn in my lap, the black-gray rain clouds of February gathering in the short dusk, I knew only the immediacy of action, the great swell of urge.

Watching the shoppers and their wares that day in the great hollow vault of the Valley Fair mall, and knowing that each had been made a promise and that the promise would be dead in their shopping bags when they got home, I heard only too well Blob's plan for my life. So, I left my mother, my dead father, and my home place because of these promises, and because in Russia, I knew, everyone already knew the promises were lies. There it was all Castle Keep and Shakespeare's history plays, the lies as big and bright as the red star of the East that would hang over my new life. I wanted to live in a country that was black and white, as black and white and grainy as the films I saw from the war my father fought. I wanted to live in a country where what people carried were the secret things in their hearts. I wanted to live in a country where one fairly new pair of shoes, brown and cracked and utilitarian, could still be a wonder.

So, yes, I did leave because I was seventeen and naive and

impulsive. I still believed life capable of great revisions then. But I don't regret leaving, cannot regret my one and only life.

2.

My first novel was *A Thousand Floating Coins*, and it has remained my most popular work. When I arrived in Moscow, I had two or three chapters of the book with me, chapters I'd written in San Jose, but I quickly tossed those pages under the guidance of my Kremlin appointed mentor, I. Zhurkin, prolific poet and novelist, twenty years my senior, exceedingly well read in the world's literatures. His two lessons during the writing of my first novel were the most important lessons, the basics. Call each character or thing by its name, and then stick to that name, he taught me; also, remove every word that can be. I had never met another writer, and I paid attention—one has to pay attention to Zhurkin, he demands it. For every word I put in black, I made another white.

A Thousand Floating Coins was published to great fanfare when I was nineteen. It should come as no surprise my first novel is the story of an American high school student who becomes disillusioned with the empty promises of capitalist life while lounging around the pool of his stepfather's condo and mourning his dead Navy father—"the sun broke golden on the surface of the pool, a thousand floating coins." The novel's hero, Richard McManus, seeks escape from America's "stifling miasma of prosperity," as one critic called it, through drugs, petty crimes, and loud music. The "miasma" becomes ever more stifling until the day Richard meets a shy but strong classmate, Selinda Roderick. Selinda's from a wealthy family who oppose Richard, she rebels against them, and the two lovers spend evenings in a night-soaked apricot orchard, bathed in pleasure and talking for hours about the fate of mankind. The two devise a plot to steal Richard's stepfather's Krugerrands, but the caper turns sour, and Richard dies heroically under the wheels of the stepfather's Montego while saving the one true thing in this world, the fair Selinda.

The novel's heroine was based on a girl I'd gone to school with, whom I adored but was too shy to speak to. The novel's tone and structure owe a good deal to American protest novels and dramas of the Thirties.

I wrote *A Thousand Floating Coins* here in Café Zhelanye, where I have written each of my nineteen books. Before Moscow I had never been to a café, we had no such beasts in San Jose in 1974, although I understand America is now a café-nation. Zhelanye is a large spare, square room of a café, with picture windows along Radzinsky Street. Rough wooden tables, simple chairs, and until not that long ago, portraits of those Soviet leaders currently in favor. Before the revolution, Zhelanye, housed on the ground floor of the Paris Hotel, had been for decades Moscow's most exclusive furrier. It was transformed into a people's café, where the revolution could be carried out on a daily basis—coffee and tea, vodka and beer, meat and bread and cheese. Today Zhelanye is pretty much the same as it's been for eighty years, except that photographs of Mikail Bulgakov, Bob Marley, and the old sixties joke, Lennon and Groucho, have replaced the past. The music has changed, too; mostly martial music slowly gave way to western pop ditties. The staffs have come and gone, as have regimes of regulars; I've been the constant these twenty-six years. Zhelanye is the still place I made for myself. It is where I learned to be alone among others, learned the habit of writing.

I came upon Zhelanye quite by accident, on my first free day here. During the long submarine voyage from San Francisco, up through the Bering Straits and under the Arctic, I was continually but rather gently debriefed by a small gang of KGB officials. While these men were somewhat chagrinned by my defection, they did not find me wanting in earnestness, and I was finally brought ashore in Leningrad, then transported via secured railcar to the Kremlin for further questioning. I liked being on the submarine, it offered me something of my father's undersea life.

The Soviet officials assigned to me were quite interested in Blob's Blue Box background, but they soon realized I had nothing to tell them. I don't remember much of these men except their crisp uniforms, cap-shaded eyes, the cloying smiles that sometimes surfaced, and the starched English they spoke. Affable, but something short of intimate.

For the next several weeks I was ensconced in a luxury apartment within the Kremlin, no windows, one guarded door. I was prize and suspect both. The apartment reminded me of the imaginary hotel room in "2001." I answered questions, received indoctrination to Soviet thought and life, ate like French royalty.

While I was confined, if ever so gently, to the Kremlin in those weeks, I did make my way around it, accompanied, of course. I met Brehznev, his Arts deputy, and Anatoly Bursk, the short and non-descript president of the Writers Congress. Brehznev did not look well, but neither did any of the top echelon of the Soviet leadership that I encountered. Much has been written about those ailing Soviets who appeared in public and rumored to be already dead—were they robots, doubles? I had been to Disneyland, sat through Great Moments with Mr. Lincoln and witnessed the animatronic wonders of dead presidents. Brehznev & Co. were not robots or doubles, they were simply sick and dying old men, but the state of their health mattered little to me. I had not come to Russia for them, for the powerful, and I was savvy enough to know that I meant little to them except that I was a piece, if only minor, in the chess game they played with their sick and dying American counterparts.

Near the end of my Kremlin stay, on a terrifically cold and barren March day, I was invited to join Brehznev & Co. on the viewing platform above Red Square for a parade in celebration of yet another anniversary of the Revolution. It was a truly awesome sight, I must say, the phalanxes of missile-laden tanks, the sharp march of the battalions, the girls and boys in native dress with baskets of flower petals, the horribly moving music. Stirring, deeply stirring, despite my attempts to resist; at baseball games in the U.S., even the American national anthem could make me cry. I was in tears that day. Brehznev whispered to the translator, who in turn whispered to me, "Just wait until May Day, now there's a parade." The procession halted briefly—a squadron of girls and boys—and all eyes turned to the viewing platform. Brehznev, *Comrade* Brehznev, turned to me—the eyes of Russia were on me—presented me with my Soviet passport, saluted me, hugged me twice, said a few words in Russian, hugged me again, then signaled the parade to recommence. I did not see Brehznev again until he died and lay in state.

On March 23, I was turned out of the Kremlin, a free citizen of the Union of Soviet Socialist Republics, and a fully-vested member of the Writers Congress. My new life had been planned to the last detail. At first I was told that I would live in the most luxurious fashion, as befitting my heroic contribution to the Revolution. A three-bedroom penthouse overlooking the river and close to the Kremlin, with an airy studio nearby for my literary work. My own car and driver. I protested vehemently, no, this was not why I had defected. Give me the People's life, let me be a part of the struggle to create the future. Looking back, it may be that their first offer to me was a test, but if so, I passed without study. I was genuine. After a brief huddle of interrogators, I was given a slightly revised life and a much smaller apartment. My chauffeur was re-assigned. My interrogators seemed more relieved than perplexed at my request for a simpler life. Perhaps the life of luxury I had spurned would go to one of them.

Still, they insisted I was to be driven to my new apartment, but I begged off that privilege, too, wishing instead to find my way through the streets of Moscow alone among my Comrades. Dressed against the tundra cold in my loden cashmere overcoat, official uniform of the Writers Congress, a coat I still own but no longer wear in public, I wandered the grand boulevards and the warren maze of alleys. I was being followed, I knew and felt, and that was fine, there was a danger of my getting lost. The map I'd been given was hopeless, many of the streets and buildings it described would not be completed for another five years, and it was being lost in this bright future that led me to the Café Zhelanye. One wrong turn to find my future, the real future, which was a bit shabby, tattered.

I sat down in Zhelanye, ordered my first Kava, unprepared for the short coffee with its floating grounds, but pleased nonetheless.

I stayed for two hours, and would have stayed until closing, but I had an appointment to meet my official translator, who was waiting for me three blocks away in my new apartment, waiting to unveil the other portion of my future.

No. 13 Nashchokinsky Street is a cramped studio, a fourth floor walk-up. Its one window overlooks a sandy courtyard of trash bins and faded children's toys, then as now. A large bed fills a closet at one end of the apartment, a big table the other, two reading chairs in what little space is left, a brief kitchen wedged against one wall. Impoverished for America, rather grand for Moscow. For many years only the two of us lived here. No. 13 has changed little since I first moved in, changed in the ways all Moscow apartments have changed, the portraits of Lenin & Co. have come down, and it takes much longer to get the plumbing fixed.

I was only a teenager, and this was my first apartment. When I walked in the door that day I laughed aloud. Freedom. I reached out to the air, as if to test the illusion, and then Jana, coming out of the water closet, spoke to me.

"This is a beautiful thing, Comrade," she said in her perfect English. "You must always cherish it, no?"

Jana Stepanova. My official translator, literary and otherwise, for all time assigned to my person and the confusions of language and idiom. My wife and the mother of our son, Allie, short for Alexander. Jana Stepanova, Johnnie her American name.

She was twenty-two that first day at No. 13., a recent graduate of the Translators Corps with a keen affinity for American literature. Her thesis, *The Dusky Hills,* concerned Steinbeck's use of adjectives. Those who'd ordered the outline of my new life must have chosen Jana rather happily; how obvious it must have seemed, given the situation, that we would fall in love, and I might be kept very busy. The inexorable weight of Jana's past, the drama of my defection, and the larger histories that contained them both all converged at No. 13.

Jana was wearing her official Translators Corps uniform, and that is how I will always see her. Soviet loden wool knee-length skirt, pastel green blouse with chevrons, black chunky low heels. Her cashmere overcoat and fur cap, with its red star patch, were placed neatly on one of our chairs. Black dossier under one arm, she stood neatly at attention. A big girl, by which I mean solid and voluptuous both, two inches taller than me, nearly six-feet. Lips, beautiful lips.

"Comrade," she said, "welcome to the revolution," and she sat me down at the table, opened the dossier of my life. For lunch she made a meal of cheese, bread, and meat, and my first taste of vodka. She taught me how to slam my glass down on the table, swear love for the motherland. She smoked relentlessly and asked me questions about America; she knew much more about America than I did, and I tasted my first cigarette. The sky slowly brightened and a meager trace of warmth filtered into the apartment. When she leaned over the table to kiss me, I asked her if this were part of her assignment, not that I cared.

No, she told me, and I believed her and let her teach me how to kiss. Lips, lips, lips, and the first soft slip of her tongue. On such moments of stupid faith, we make our lives.

I was seventeen and had only kissed a few girls. Later in bed that first day, while I fumbled, feigning experience, Jana told me to stop. "You," she said, "you just lie down and I will show you two or three things," and she did. Her most valuable piece of advice that day, "if you don't know what you're doing, please do not do it harder."

Jana was not a virgin. One did not rise, she told me, in the Soviet Union without some compromises, Kompromat. She hadn't objected to the men, her superiors, who had slept with her. She was young and curious, mildly ambitious.

While the sun faded that evening and we tried to rouse ourselves from our sleepy bed to attend another official dinner, I asked Jana one more question of faith. Was I another rung on her ladder? She understood the idiom. "No, silly boy," she said. "I am here because I know you are not trying to steal my secrets."

e⁓

The larger tide of history swept Jana and me into a private eddy of chance and fortune. We reveled in our seclusion. Jana needed a shelter from the claim of history that would strip her of her every secret, dragging her bare bones along its swift narrow canyon; needed a world where her secrets would not be stolen from her, where she could only give them freely, or keep them. I needed a place where all secrets were visible to me, where you could spot the players by their costumes, know to stay away from the man in the black hat. No. 13 was our eddy, safe from history, or so we thought, with the constant roar of it still drumming in our ears.

I did not desert America for Revolution, although at first I believed I had. I'd left for exile, the writer's only possible condition.

And so, Jana and I immediately settled into a rigid routine, one we held for fourteen years. Each morning I wrote at Zhelanye, while Jana went to the Corps and worked over news items from American and British papers, then we'd meet at No. 13 for lunch and spend the afternoons translating and typing my novels into her reputedly crystalline Russian. Through the early evening we made love and read to each other from an unlimited supply of literature in English, courtesy the KGB. At eight or nine we almost always went out for a supper with writer friends, officially and otherwise.

Our circle of these friends were mostly older writers from the Congress who'd adopted me, and I learned a good deal about writing from these men and women, especially from Zhurkin. He was tough on me, determined, and in this way, he's still a bit of a bastard, and dearest friend. "If you do not put your everything into your next book," he said one drunken evening, "every drop of your blood, I will hunt you down and beat your sweet pumpkin head with a silver stick." He taught me to refrain from excess, to write quickly, avoid pronouncements. He also taught me that all great literature is essentially comic, that it must make us guffaw as we weep. "All else," he said on another, more drunken evening, "is mere trickery, showmanship, a plea to be loved for one's own sensitivity. No one cares about the writer, only the written."

Grigorov, Nashtun, Treuth, Nevsky, his daughter Lyuba, Timirov, many others. Typically we'd gather at an apartment we hadn't been to in a while, a supper of bread, cheese, and meat, and miraculous bottles of vodka and cognac, tart Hungarian wine. No one had any money to go out, and we were safe in our homes. We were official writers, and as such, were offered leeway in our discourse. Though we knew that we were often followed or bugged, we knew that we were safe enough to drink and talk with it on our tongues. I have never learned, all these years, to hold my vodka, or any other alcohol, and was never able to keep up with Jana and our friends. I often missed the most heated moments of our discussions; Jana would tell me all about them the next day. Early in this part of our lives, I was given the Russian nickname Coat Rack after I was found one ragged middle of the night asleep under a pile of coats in the bottom of Timirov's closet.

We talked about literature. I listened for many years. Loud music, mostly western, lots of dancing. One hasn't truly lived, I believe, until one has seen Zhurkin the Stork flail to the Rolling Stones. We read our work, traded books, and read aloud what would have been forbidden in print. Our own little Samizdat circle. The raging beauty I heard there, the calamitous circus of life, disappeared, evaporated unheeded. We stood on the stage of the world, but the doors to the theater were locked to our audience. At the end of each reading, the writer would toss the manuscript into the fireplace or stuff it into a small stove.

We spoke mostly English these evenings. I have yet to learn enough Russian to fill a tea cup, and the others all wanted to practice their English, preparing for the day they would defect to the west—ah, Vasily, Tatyana, where are you now? Only as the evening dragged on and the bottles emptied would we switch to Russian, which I never minded. I loved to drown in the dark gurgle of the Russian tongue.

Jana herself was often the star on a given night. Jana wrote slyly, in the best two senses of the word, wickedly and secretly. No one outside of our circle knew that she wrote, and she never tried to publish. Her stories were out from under Gogol's "Overcoat," faithfully so, stories filled with the vanities and follies of ass-kissing Soviet officials of middling rank, the men and women she worked under. She was tender with these characters, reminding us that the buffoons were, in the end, merely humans wading through a world become grotesquely complex. Jana might work for months on a story, refining her drafts on the backs of translations she'd done at work that day. She wrote in English, and she would read them to me privately first, breathless and intent, still working over the story. When she read for Zhurkin and the others, she read clearly and honestly, her back straight, military, only a glimpse of smile over the most wicked passages. When she was done, she'd toss the manuscript into the fire before we had a chance to recover from our stunned silences. Whoosh, up in flames. Manuscripts *do* burn.

I have no idea if Jana still writes stories, and if she does, what they might concern.

ℰ

I have written nothing about Russia until now. My eyes, my heart, and my memory, were always trained on America, by official arrangement. Once a week, a KGB officer would come by No. 13 with a horde of American books, magazines, and newspapers, taking away the previous week's carefully inventoried supply. And once a month, Jana and I were invited into a cramped room in an anonymous office building for a viewing of American films, television shows, and news reports, a viewing that might last twelve hours. Lavish meals provided. Jana was allowed to attend so that she might improve her command of American slang.

We watched, over the years, America's willful descent into an amnesia to which I knew it was already prone. Our favorite phrase: Ski Heavenly Today. Such a Soviet phrase, really. The goal of America, it seemed to Jana and me, was to provide extreme recreational activities. Television commercials showed us that, books were no better. Escape.

Except for my first weeks here, I was never homesick, and those first moments of longing were, I knew even then, nothing more severe than the longing I would have felt had I gone off to college in Santa Barbara.

What I did miss. The flowering plums of February, the biting lime-green of spring's wild grasses, the bent and twisted beauty of oak trees against a gray-black rain sky, the slanted gold of perfect afternoons on the coast. I missed California, the California of my childhood, when we were all still together. I missed my father, all those years.

❧

Züünbaya-Ulaan is a rural outpost an eleven-hour jeep ride southwest of Ulaanbaatar, the capital of Mongolia. I was visiting Mongolia in 1989 on a cultural exchange, giving readings and participating in workshops, when Jana and Allie disappeared to America. I did not discover they had left until my return to Moscow.

Züünbaya-Ulaan is a scant collection of odd, squat buildings in the middle of a vast sea of windy steppe, nothing for miles but leagues of grass over the swells of rolling hills, and to the north, an endless fence of green mountains. On the evening that Jana and Allie left Moscow, a tepid and hazy evening in Züünbaya-Ulaan, I was to give a reading from *A Thousand Floating Coins* in the town's Soviet hall. The audience for the reading had been arriving all day from outlying settlements, and outside the Soviet hall, a herd of motorcycles and horses had gathered. The Soviet hall, plywood walls and packed dirt floor, was crowded with families dressed in their finest *dels*. I was moved that so many people had come so far to hear a reading, by me or any other writer.

What I remember most about the readings in Mongolia are the silences both during and after. My Mongolian translator, Bagabandi, explained this silence to me after the first reading of the tour. "Our people," he told me, "live in great silent places," and he swept his arm across an imaginary steppe. "All our news of the outside world comes through the short-wave radio, we are so far away, we have learned to listen with great intent, afraid of missing one singular word. Please do not find yourself insulted by our many quietudes." I was not insulted, in fact, came to desire this silence from all my audiences.

The format of the Mongolian readings was a bit strange, as it had to be, my Mongolian being non-existent, except for *please, thank you, where,* and *coffee*. I would read the opening page of *A Thousand Floating Coins* in English, then sit down while Bagabandi stood and read the entire first chapter in Mongolian. Perhaps I had gone into exile for precisely such moments, to escape the onslaught of a language laden with the traps of meaning, and to revel in the pristine song of a foreign tongue. After the reading that night in Züünbaya-Ulaan, the silence was a great balloon that crowded out all other sounds. Bagabandi, turning from the crowd, smiled wide as the sky.

During the obligatory question and answer period that followed, and which I'm sure all writers detest, as does most of the audience, the questions were the most clear-headed I'd ever been asked. What is an apricot, what type of soil is best, how is irrigation achieved in the Santa Clara Valley, is there truly a place so fertile it can support such bounty?

During a reception with local brews and cuisine, the Soviet hall slowly filled with the chatter of my gracious hosts, but I craved the silence that had been created earlier, and I slipped outside, making my way through the knot of buildings that was Züünbaya-Ulaan, and escaped the noose of the settlement's two streetlights. A rain of stars assaulted me, threatened to melt me back to earth. Then the roaring silence filled the space, a vast battle of silence swept along by the hollow winds and the hush of the grassy hills. Though I did not know it, Jana had just left Moscow, on the way to Paris, on the way to Barbuda, and from there, America. Jana had taken Allie with her, Alexander, our one year old.

There was a note waiting for me on the scarred table in No. 13 when I returned from Mongolia.

Robert, I do understand why you are unable to come back to America. But for Allie, yes? His future. I love you, and Allie will, too. J.

The note was attached to a case lot of the official Writers Congress notebooks I had always used, green with red stars, more than enough for a lifetime. She'd also left a box of ink refills and a spare pen.

I immediately went to Zhelanye and drank vodka until Zhurkin found me there. "Come, my little Coat Rack," he said, "it's home for you."

After Jana got pregnant, we had long discussions about

whether to leave Moscow, perhaps go to Europe, but Jana's eye was always on America, and after Allie was born, these discussions intensified. Virtually every night of the one near-year I had with Allie, Jana spoke of leaving. She truly understood why I did not want to return to America, and I understood why Jana wanted to go there, and Allie in his crib, on our laps, in his pram, served to both distract and compel our arguments. But I could not go. *Was not able to*, Jana would surely correct. I had already had enough. Mom and Blob were dead by this time, killed in a freak jet-ski accident at Lake Havasu, and any friends or cousins who might remember me had dispersed into widespread corporate ghettos—Houston, Atlanta, Sacramento.

The Thaw, of course, had already begun in Russia, and it was no longer possible to ignore the creaking of the ice cap of Soviet rule, the rending of that great expanse into smaller and smaller floes, the dangers inherent in disparity. Jana had only ever known the Soviet Union; without it, in a new Russia, she would surely freeze and drown. She had been too official.

It was Zhurkin who discovered Jana's escape route. Two weeks after my return to Moscow, he flew into No. 13 and threw a video cassette at my feet. I was already quite drunk, in fact I was reaching the end of the day's first drunk and about to take a nap so that I could rise at dusk and begin the next. I was sitting in my reading chair with a bottle of vodka and staring at Allie's empty crib.

Zhurkin also brought with him his newest prize, a small television set with a built-in VCR, an item whose source he refused to divulge. Poet and spy, that Zhurkin, one in the same, always had been. He said nothing that day, popped in the tape, grabbed the vodka, and sat on the floor at my feet.

The tape told a story that was becoming increasingly familiar at the time, Russians selling themselves. Russian video brides, a simple arrangement. American men, discreet gentlemen of means, as the tape would have it, after viewing a given tape, would choose a Russian woman as a prospective bride and negotiate to meet her on the island of Barbuda at a private resort there. The men paid for everything in the deal, airfare and lodging for their "bride," every minute of time spent with the "ladies," gifts for their "escorts." For some of the men, the service was nothing more than exotic prostitution; others actually purchased brides.

Jana was shown in her interview already on the beach in Barbuda, but the viewers were told they would have to pay her airfare from Russia. It was obvious that no one was choosing any one "bride," that the American men would simply arrive on Barbuda and make their arrangements with the women stabled there. No one seemed to object to the smoke and mirrors. These men, Zhurkin and I figured, were spending at least ten thousand dollars each for a week of sex with women who had been spurned by history. These men had moved beyond logic, had accepted jagged illusions, and showed a supreme willingness to disbelieve.

Imagine what it must have been like for me to watch Jana's interview, the faux broken English she was forced to use, the body which had been my life. She is standing on a beach at sunset, speaking directly to the camera. She is already someone else. The quality of the video is intentionally amateurish, the colors grainy and brash.

"I am called Jana Stepanova. I am so attractive, charming, easy, energy, gentle-loving, sexy-tender, with broad sense of humor. You will communicate me to my home address. I wait for messages."

Jana's hair is dyed gold and black, a bad shag. She is haunted and tanned. Purpled pink nails, blue eye shadow. The look she concocts for the camera: get me out of here.

Zhurkin stayed on Jana's trail for a full year or more; I was too drunk and ashamed, in the beginning, to do so myself. It had been quite easy, it turned out, for Jana to arrange her defection. A girlfriend from her schooldays introduced Jana to the bridal agency, and she was immediately secured as a client, paying for her inclusion with jewels that had been in her family since before the Revolution. Between the agency's cash and Jana's contacts in different government bureaus, she'd had little trouble arranging a special visa. Jana and Allie flew to Paris, then on to Barbuda.

Zhurkin discovered that three weeks after her arrival there, Jana, who had obtained a divorce without my knowing it, married Tod Coeur, a forty-seven year-old orthopedic surgeon from Yakima, Washington. Jana was Tod's second wife, and while he had three nearly grown children of his own, he rarely saw them and welcomed Allie as his own. Jana had discovered America.

⁓

I eventually stopped drinking vodka for breakfast, returned to my writing, and had Allie's crib removed from No. 13. I rarely spoke with anyone other than Zhurkin during the first year, and no longer went out at night; I slowly recovered and reclaimed my Russian life.

My life has stayed much the same; it's the world that's changed. The Soviets fell, and America has crept in here, but only in the most insidious ways. The official lies are no longer quite as visible, hidden as they are beneath the cloak of infinitely possible self-betterment. In truth, the gangsters have taken over, and will as soon kill you as give up one measly ruble. Russia is now America.

My fiction is still published and read, and perhaps as it's always been read, not for the "scathing" portrait of prosperity's empty promises, but for the empty promises themselves. Publication is not the grand event it once was; with the Writers Congress dissolved, the stacks of white and green paperbacks no longer preen in official store windows. In place of state publishing, small journals and publishers financed by the wealthy and aspiring, handfuls of copies. Electronic magazines, ephemera. Literature, it turns out, is now nearly dead in Russia, too.

I still go to Zhelanye every morning to write, and in the afternoons I type my drafts and leave them outside my door, but for tattooed motorcycle couriers rather than KGB. My work, as before, appears only in Russian translation. I've published a shelf's worth of books, all of them strangers to me.

The most drastic change in my writing life—perhaps in all of my life—was a swift and immediate conversion to the short story. I had only ever written three short stories, everything else was novels. I devoured the short story as a reader, heavy on both Russians and Americans, but felt ridiculous writing stories in Chekhov's motherland.

When I returned from Mongolia to find Jana and Allie gone, I wrote nineteen short stories in a feverish and drunken six weeks, all about American fathers exiled from their children, terse and alarming stories, knife-edged, at least to me while I was writing them. I didn't take up the form; it swamped me. I've written nothing but short stories since.

It is simple enough to figure why I've taken up the form so ferociously. The novel concerns memory, memory in motion, the mind in motion through memory, flowing out of the character's life like a six thousand mile river. The novel describes the past, yearns for it, and yet with all its backward turning, the novel still does imply the future. When I came to Russia, I left behind an ocean of memory I could tap forever. Rivers and rivers of novels, floating downstream into the past. The future is always upstream.

The short story is the still place, that one bright moment where the world makes itself known to the character. The short story is the tiny, exposed beach at the bend in the river where the character sits until he realizes, if only in the last moment of the story, that he is still part of the river, no matter how diligently he has resisted the dark water's pull.

Sitting on the beach of the short story these last eleven years has not been as confining it might seem. I've finally stopped writing about America. I'm writing about Russia for the first time; no, not Russia, but Russians, my neighbors. In part, because of the story form itself, stuck in the moment, and because I've gotten to know my neighbors in new ways. This, too, because of the short story form, it turns out.

I was, of course, in the pay of the Soviets, through a sort of royalty system, but let's be honest, they kept me. They did sell my novels, but when the Soviet publishing structure collapsed, replaced by ad hoc at best, I committed what has to be considered suicide for a writer in the best of times, I turned to short stories. At least novels offer the possibility of money. To make ends meet, I took up other work. I give English lessons now, and I write letters in English on behalf of those Muscovites struggling with the immigration bureaucracy of the United States. I've sat in rooms for hours with my neighbors and talked to them about their lives. That has been a great help.

Jana, too, has helped, I will say that much. Eleven months after their exile, near Allie's birthday, I received my first letter from her, and we have continued to write each other. Between us, we have made a peace. I asked to come, but was refused; I was asked to come, and I refused; many years the notion never arose. By our agreement, Allie did not know about me until he could figure it out himself, about three years ago.

Jana has kept me apprised of Allie's life. She often includes a drawing of his, or a piece of homework. She sends photos with every letter. She makes that effort.

The walls of No. 13 are thick with proof of his life. Allie has his mother's lips, always has, but as he's grown he has taken on the likeness of my father, his eyes particularly, and the proud way he holds his shoulders. For the last four years, most of the photos have Allie dressed in a baseball uniform. He's a good kid, I can tell that from her letters, smart. Funny, she says, goofy.

I have spent a good deal of my life trying to imagine what Allie is like, how his hand would feel in mine if he would still hold it. But I can't. The only photos of Allie that awaken him bodily in me are two from before he was erased from my life. The first is Allie at two weeks, my hand covers his entire torso, he's asleep, the way we used to nap together late mornings when he was an infant.

The second is Allie at eleven months, and we're in the first Moscow McDonald's. Zhurkin took the photo a few weeks before

I last saw Allie. I'm wearing my green writer's coat, Allie's wearing a little fur coat that Jana somehow appropriated for him. He has just learned to stand, on the verge of walking, and he's holding on to my fingers; I'm sitting on a red plastic chair at a yellow plastic table, and in the background, hundreds of Russians are waiting for their Happy Meals. Both Allie and I are laughing, our heads thrown back. I remember why we are laughing. I have just called him "squid boy" in English, and something about the sound of the words or the way in which I say them is making Allie laugh, and I'm laughing with him, delighted that we can create such a fine place. I do not think I have ever been happier.

The latest photo of Allie shows him again in his baseball uniform. Nearly twelve now, dramatically taller, he's adopted the self-seriousness of professional athletes and all other adolescents. In the letter with the photo was my first note from Allie, typed on his word processor, signed with a green pen and confident hand. He would like to meet me.

I've made the arrangements. I will fly to Sakhalin, from there to Seattle, then one last flight to Yakima. In all my travels, I will not have made my way around the world, I have skipped Europe and the Atlantic, a fact that seems oddly fitting. I am coming home.

3.

This is the perfect moment, the one-shot that will play for twenty-four hours then disappear forever. The father returns to his lost homeland for his son. Cameras and microphones swarm the arrival gate, starved for the one-shot, they must capture my tears, steal the one sentence that defines the moment. But there are no cameras or mics at the arrival gate at SeaTac International, nor in Yakima where I am one of seven fagged out passengers crawling into the weary, haze-speckled day. Only a hotel limo waits for me.

The streets of Yakima are broad and empty, as clean as in a dream. It's all shopping from here to Tallahassee, beige stucco facades that are a combination of the Alamo and the Alhambra. Acres of parking. The neighboring houses seem the spawn of the stores.

What most disconcerts me is the landscape behind the regulation architecture, Yakima and its surroundings. The rolling steppes of hills swathed in spring green, endless except the wall of mountains in the west, it all reminds me not so much of America as of Mongolia. And under the preening whine of the automobiles, or perhaps defined by their meager sound, I hear, too, the vast silence of Mongolia, the silence and its attendant roar.

I check into the Best Western Yakima Heights, beige stucco and faux imperial, and fall asleep in an immaculate bed, and when I awake near midnight, what I hear is the howling of the wind.

Jana calls the next morning and asks me to meet her at her salon, Johnnie's Hair and Nails. She is Johnnie here, but I still call her Jana. Her voice is the same, crisp and deep, but some of her Russian tones have disappeared, flat vowels have intruded, and in this change I hear her age, she's forty-eight now, as if she's grown tired of struggle and has conceded some basic parts of herself, her defenses. We talk as if not much has changed, as if we're making plans to meet at Zhelanye or Zhurkin's. She wishes to speak privately before I meet Allie.

There are no taxis here in Yakima, none that I can find, but the hotel has arranged a limo again, free of charge, yesterday's driver again, Mr. Ghassan. I cannot help but wonder if all of America is like this now, cramped taxis gone and everyone chauffeured like moguls. Mr. Ghassan is the father of five and dresses in a sparkling black suit. He loves his job, he tells me, and is still stunned by the verdure of Yakima after three years here. "Look," he says, sweeping his arm across the horizon, "how could anyone starve here?"

Johnnie's Hair and Nails is on the front edge of a brand new mini-mall, The Shops at Brookview Terrace. The Shops, pink and beige stucco, are surrounded by a tract of three-car homes, also pink and beige stucco, that look as if they've never been lived in. The trees are still twigs. In the mall, Borders, The Gap, a French cheese store, a French bakery, The House of Smoked Salmon, three coffee shops, two sporting goods outlets. My first thought is angry and Russian. "In Moscow," I say to Mr. Ghassan, "we are happy to find one can of tinned meat and a roll of toilet paper."

"But you are not Russian," he says.

I touch the red star on the lapel of my green writer's coat.

It's still early and the parking lot is empty, except for a green BMW that must be Jana's. Mr. Ghassan parks across several spaces, and through my tinted window I spy Jana. She is perched on the high chair of the station near the window, a cup of coffee held delicately in her big hands. She is in a long black wool dress, black stockings, low black boots. Her hair is short and frosted several shades of brass and copper. The makeup around her eyes is blue, a little too heavy, her lips are peachy. I could never have imagined her like this. Jana has spotted the limo and is sitting up straight now. I push the button that lowers the window, and we are smiling at each other in the bright morning.

Jana unlocks the salon door, and we embrace there, three kisses on the cheeks, as in Moscow. We hold each other close on the last kiss, letting go with a laugh. The shop is all mirrors, white porcelain, and chrome, austere. I take the coffee she has for me, a double latté, of all things, and we sit in the big chairs. I have never tasted anything as rich as this coffee.

Make no mistake, I would fuck her right here in the window of the salon.

It's not too awkward, our catching up. Moscow friends, my writing, the trip here, my hotel. Allie's school, how the shop is doing. She likes doing hair, it's been good for her English.

When Jana speaks of Allie, she is the Jana I once knew, no secrets. And then and then, she says, and all I can do is listen. She makes a strenuous point of telling me that Allie loves to write stories, that he has some imagination.

She glances at the clock.

"I am sorry, Robert," she says. "I did what had to be done, for Allie, you know that. I just wanted to tell you in person, I am sorry."

Before she can continue, I put up my hand against what she will say next. She smiles and blows on her coffee. We move on.

Tod would like me to come for dinner, she says, and I know that the gesture is genuine, but I can't accept. I'm dying to see Allie's room, see their home, but I'm not ready for that. I'd like to see Allie alone now, watch him play ball as we'd planned. We'll see.

Someone is knocking on the window, a young woman, stylishly dressed, who can only be described as thin, and she seems to be having some sort of crisis. "Johnnie," she cries when Jana opens the door. "Look," the woman says, holding out a hand that seems beautiful and perfect. Jana looks at the hand, clucks. The woman looks at me with an expression that betrays bafflement. She enters the shop and sits at one of the low nail stations, nursing her hand.

Jana steps outside with me. The day is suddenly warm, and the limo makes its way across the parking lot with regal ponderousness. Jana points to the horizon. "You know the address, yes? It's up there," she says, "where we live, on the farthest ridge. It's a very nice house." She kisses me three times and returns to her shop.

❧

Mr. Ghassan drives me around Yakima all day, from one cluster of stores to another. I am looking for a gift for Allie, a gift that must be special, unique, one he will always cherish and remind him of me. I am being sentimental, yes, but this day will never come again. At some of the shopping plateaus, the stores are rather distant from one another, and Mr. Ghassan insists we drive, but I'd rather walk, and he accompanies me on these long treks over the hot asphalt. The sky is awash with high, feathery clouds; my skin tingles.

A few years back, Zhurkin took a trip to London. A British publisher was preparing a volume of his selected poems. When he returned Zhurkin spoke not of his poetry nor the bits of history he'd seen in London, but of the shops. He had been overwhelmed, nearly fainted, when his editor took him to the Virgin Megastore. "Such things," he had cried to me, "so many such things. You cannot know. I had hoped to find one CD of Ben Webster, but there was an entire Ben Webster section." Zhurkin had had to close his eyes for a moment, to still himself, and even then, he told me, he was overwhelmed by the incessant clacking of the plastic CD cases. "I left with nothing," he said. I had heard other such stories from Russian friends who'd visited the west. Nevsky's daughter had literally fainted in the detergent aisle of a San Francisco Safeway. It wasn't the emotions of the moment, she'd told me, it was the fumes, too much Tide.

I am an American, or had been, and I should be prepared for what I am seeing with Ghassan, but I'm not. In O.G. Toyz, I am stunned to silence by the rows upon rows of plastic and electronic gizmos. Gizmos seems the only word for these products, complex machines with one aim. They hardly seem capable of unleashing either play or pleasure. There's The Detonator, a plastic saucer with a display of lights that, when activated, blink in a certain sequence; the object of the game is to match the sequence, failure to do so resulting in the destruction of the game itself. The Detonator is very expensive, and seems in its single-mindedness an apt fit for the autistic. I hold the toy, and its lights mesmerize me.

Later, in yet another parking lot, Mr. Ghassan offers to help. "Video games," he says. "Buy your son a video game, he will admire you for it no matter what. If he has it, he can exchange it, especially if he does not have the proper operating system. I understand this will be disappointing to you, that such a gift must seem only cash in disguise. What are we do to? Kids, ho, I tell you."

I want to buy Allie a wooden train, Lincoln Logs—things that travel, things that build, toys from my past, what I was never able to give him.

In another store, Mr. Ghassan points me to Legos, claims boys Allie's age and much older still play with them, but the Lego sets on display, like all the toys in Yakima, build only one thing, do not combine with other sets, and are all figures from movies I haven't seen. I admit finally that I know nothing of my son—is he right or left handed; how can I buy him a new baseball glove?—and I break down and buy him a video game. Death Team, two to four players. It's the most expensive of the games, brand new, and I pay full price.

Mr. Ghassan drops me off at the Best Western, and we make arrangements to meet at four. I seem to be his sole concern. Passing through the lobby I drop Death Team on the one of the loveseats there. Another man's treasure. I will give Allie a watch instead, a watch presented to me by the Mongolian Writers Congress. The watch is clunky, stainless steel with a leather strap, on its face the Mongolian flag, and below that the hammer and sickle, but the hammer in this symbol has been replaced with a pen. I have never worn it.

e

Allie will be twelve in one month, and already he's nearly as tall as me. His feet are enormous, his hands, too. When he first stepped out of the house, Tod's house, and walked to me down the sloped driveway, I nearly burst into hilarious laughter, but I managed to hold back. Here he was at last, in front of me, my son.

A few months before Allie was born, I had a dream of him,

he seemed to be three or so in the dream, and he was a little man, not a child; that is, he was full-grown in his proportions and face, but the height of a pre-schooler. He looked quite a bit like me, but more eerie was that he looked exactly like my father. He was even dressed as my father had dressed, khaki pants and a green plaid camp shirt. After the dream, I knew he'd be born healthy. That dream has come to life, Allie does look exactly like my father, and not just my father as a young man, but my father as I remember him.

I stand near the limo's open door, terrified. Jana stands in the doorway of her large home and waves a little as Allie comes down the drive in his blue and white Badgers uniform, glove and hat dangling from his wrist. The stucco of the homes on the ridge line, the steppe of grasses beyond, the pure sky, all are tinged by the long gold of the quickening afternoon. Allie smiles, but is staring at the limo, obviously impressed.

He looks right at me, then practically throws himself into my arms. I kiss his hair. The afternoon envelops us.

"Jeez, Dad," Allie says, "you sure know how to make a good impression. Man, a limo."

"It's the hotel's, Allie," I say, and the sound of his name crackles the air. "But I'm glad you like it, I'm glad I'm here."

"Oh, yes, Dad," he says. He does now what's always tritely imagined at such moments. He throws his arms around me and starts to cry. I'm crying, too.

Allie turns to Jana, we both wave to her, and clamber into the back of the limo. Mr. Ghassan's gleaming eyes catch mine in the rearview mirror, then he raises the privacy window, sealing us—me and my son!—in our own little cabin.

"So, Allie," I say.

"So, Dad."

"So, Allie."

"Let's just pretend, for now, that you're my dad and I'm your son and we're going to my baseball game."

Allie pauses, then pulls an astonished face.

"In a *limo*," he says, falling back, and we're both laughing.

We eat at a restaurant called Home'n'Hearth, a chain whose decor is American kitsch—maple hutches, apple dolls, butter churns—an America of New England, three thousand miles distant, and one that surely never existed. But I like the way the restaurant feels, it's cozy.

Allie explains the menu to me with great seriousness, then we talk about baseball. His team's not very good, he tells me, but he enjoys playing, especially his position, centerfield. He makes a case for centerfield as a crucial position, inflates his prowess a bit. "Mostly," he says, "I like standing out there. Night games especially, with the lights all lit up. Did you ever play baseball, Dad?"

He can't help saying Dad over and over, the sound of the word directed at me. Perhaps, if he says it enough, the spell will work, and I'll become his real father.

Our food arrives, and I can't believe Allie will be able to eat it all—a double hamburger, cole slaw, a mountain of fries, chocolate pie, a liter of coke.

I've ordered a steak—I've been dreaming of this steak—a glass of red wine, and a shot of vodka out of habit. I raise my shot glass and say a little too loudly, "Yakima!"

"Moscow," Allie says, raising his coke.

I down the vodka and slam the shot glass on the table. The restaurant falls silent, people are staring. We are surrounded by an ocean of pale, watery beer and syrupy children's drinks.

"Toast," Allie says, and slams his coke on the table. We smile at each other, private and contained, and the restaurant gets noisy again, out of embarrassment.

We're not laughing, we're roaring, and for that moment we might as well be your average weekend divorced dad and son, relieved to be together, lost in America.

Allie and I fill up the wide spaces of the restaurant with our talk, his talk really, what he likes and doesn't, who he likes and doesn't. I try not to make any judgments, I'm simply waiting for the pieces of the picture to accrue, to build on the one year-old I have carried in my heart for so long. Allie knows too much about the film industry, who produces and who directs and how much gross is considered acceptable. He talks of sports, but doesn't seem to have a true passion for them. He's making it very easy on me. Couldn't have asked for a better kid.

In the parking lot of Hearth'n'Home, on the way to Mr. Ghassan's limo, Allie breaks my heart. He takes my hand and holds it. Then more talking all the way to the ballpark.

The Raymond Carver Memorial Recreation Field is named for a writer who went to high school in Yakima, and who, I'm sure from having read his work, never played a stitch of sports in his life. Still, a nice gesture, if it isn't all wrong in other ways—too bright, too clean, too new and too safe. It's dusk when we arrive, and I'm most incredulous of the night lighting. First, that there is such a thing for a child's game, and then by the lights themselves. The baseball diamond is sunken, ensconced in its own bowl, and while Allie and I are crossing it, the lights come blazing on, drench us, saturate us, obliterate any notions of day and night. Allie gives me a quick, wordless hug, breaking my heart for a second time in one night, then breaks into a full run, screaming towards his team.

All the parents are there, every single one it seems, and I take my place in the bleachers with them. We're all here to root.

The national anthem causes some embarrassment for me. Everyone is standing, quite solemn, the parents with their hands over their hearts, the players with their hats over their hearts, and I find myself weeping a bit, moved by the swell of the music. I have a million reasons to weep.

The evening is gorgeous, perfect, and everyone here seems to expect it. The Badgers are doing pretty well, down 7-5 in the seventh, and I can almost see in Allie's posture a kind of joy that they aren't down by more. Everybody's happy. Then the game changes when the Screaming Eagles load the bases on three solid hits, no outs. The Screaming Eagles' star pitcher, also their best hitter, a big muscle-bound kid who seems too old by years for this game, steps up to the plate, takes one warm-up swing, then launches into the first pitch. It cracks unmistakably and is on its way. We all know that if this one doesn't land in a glove, the game is pretty much over.

The ball is headed into deep center, straight at Allie, and he's backing up, way way back, but his glove stays down, the ball's thirty feet over his head at the cyclone fence and it disappears into the black night beyond.

All the while this guy next to me, an Eagles' fan no doubt, he's yelling and he's up on his feet. We're all on our feet, and this guy's yelling, the only one making a sound. He's yelling, "it's going, it's gonna go, there it goes, go, baby, go—it's history, history, history, gone, way gone, fucking history." The ball has sailed far past Allie, and the guy's still yelling.

Allie is standing against the cyclone fence, his fingers hooked in the links, he's dropped his glove. He's looking into the night as if all this might change, as if the swing and the hit could be cancelled, as if it might all come back to him out of the deep American night.